GENOCIDE

ALSO BY BRENT TOWNS

Team Reaper Thrillers

Fear the Reaper Series

The MI6 Files

Talon Series

Mark Hayes Series

Dave Nash Thrillers

Treasure Series

GENOCIDE

THE GODS OF WAR

BOOK 1

BRENT TOWNS

Genocide
Paperback Edition

Rough Edges Press
An Imprint of Wolfpack Publishing
1707 E. Diana Street
Tampa, FL 33610

roughedgespress.com

Paperback ISBN 978-1-68549-357-8
eBook ISBN 978-1-68549-356-1
LCCN 2024937401

GENOCIDE

PROLOGUE

MI6 INTERROGATION SITE, LONDON

Charles German, Christine Ryan, and Jack Holland sat across the stainless-steel desk from me and Ray Jensen. All three were members of parliament from the intelligence committee. The room was sterile, white, plain, cold. Ryan stared at us and said, "You two have been busy."

I nodded. "That's what we were employed to do."

Jensen remained quiet as he stared at her. She noticed his abnormal silence and asked, "Nothing to say?"

"Why are we being interrogated?"

"This isn't an interrogation. It's a debriefing."

"If you say so. Where is Holly Smith?"

"She is being debriefed also."

I stared at them. All were in their forties. The new brigade of politicians. Those who thought the world could be made safer by talk rather than action. "You people have no idea what we do."

"That's why we're here," German said. "We intend to get to the bottom of your illegal activities."

Jensen raised his eyebrows. "Illegal? Mate, you have no fucking idea what we did. Yet you already have made a decision."

"Language, Mr. Jensen," Christine Ryan reprimanded him.

Knocker bit back a savage retort. Like me, he was sick of people like this who were not capable of conceiving what it was that we did. "Be fucked," Jensen said with a shake of his head. "You head up intelligence and you have no idea what is going on in the world."

"We know now, but that is what we want to find out," Holland snapped.

"Then how about you sit there, shut up, and listen," I said to them. "You might just learn something."

"Then how about you tell us, Mr. Kane," Ryan said curtly.

I looked at Knocker and nodded. "All right, it started with something they called The Breath of God."

THE BREATH OF GOD

THE SYRIAN MIG-25 CAME OUT OF THE VALLEY HUGGING THE deck, causing the shimmering heatwave to part with its passage. As it passed, the sonic boom rolled across the landscape as it gained speed, the pilot pushing the throttles further forward.

"This is Scimitar One. Two minutes to target."

"Copy, Scimitar One."

Another boom sounded, shattering the once quiet terrain as the throttles were pushed further yet.

Half a mile to the east, a herd of scared goats took flight and scattered in all directions in terror of the giant bird. A young boy tried to stop them, but it was all in vain.

Inside the cockpit, the pilot checked his display and instruments, making sure everything was in order.

One minute out, he armed the weapon and prepared to drop it. Ahead of him, he could see the two hills with the valley between them. That was where his target rested.

"Weapon armed, preparing to drop."

"Copy, weapon armed."

The pilot's thumb hovered over the button, ready to depress it.

The Mig passed between the hills.

The thumb moved.

The weapon dropped.

People died.

Twenty men walked out of the wadi wearing masks and armed with AK-12s. At the head of them was their captain, Boris Chuzhkov, Special Operations Forces of the Armed Forces of the Russian Federation, commonly known as Special Operations Forces. He waved his right arm to the side, and four men broke away and jogged toward the village.

He watched them go until they disappeared. Ahead of him, Chuzhkov saw the first of the dead Kurdish villagers, inanimate lumps of flesh on the rough ground. "Scout team, report?"

"It looks like the weapon worked, Captain," came the voice over the comms.

"No survivors?"

"Not that we can find, sir."

"Scimitar Six to Sheath, over."

"Copy, Six."

"Initial reports are positive. Will update shortly."

"Copy, standing by."

The Russian captain saw a body staring up at him, wide-eyed, dried saliva present at the corners of the mouth. Chuzhkov grunted in satisfaction.

As they entered the village, more corpses presented with the same results. Men, women, and children. The weapon did not discriminate.

"Results are positive," Chuzhkov said into his radio. "Checking for residual."

"Copy."

The Russian commander reached up and removed his mask. Breathing normally, he waited. Nothing happened. One by one, the rest of his operations team did the same.

Another grunt of satisfaction and he said, "This is Scimitar Six. Residual negative. Ground zero is clear."

"Copy. Continue mission."

For the next hour, the Russian special forces team continued with their mission.

"Sir, we have found her."

Chuzhkov followed his man to where a figure lay on the ground behind a house. He stared at the body for a long time before nodding. "It is her. Get all the bodies together and burn them."

Moments later, the commander was on the radio. "This is Scimitar Six. Mission success, I say again, mission success. Out."

"Copy, mission success. Bring your people home. Out."

CHAPTER 1

ANTWERP, BELGIUM

I couldn't believe I was back in Antwerp again, working for Interpol. It was dark out, and the streetlamps cast their dull orange, reflecting off the puddles formed from the rain earlier in the evening.

People call me Reaper because of the tattoo I have on my back. I'm six-four, broad across the shoulders, and a warrior of the world. More than once, I've been called upon to rid humanity of human garbage.

I looked across the intersection from where I stood in the darkened doorway. The rounded facades of the sandstone buildings might have looked pretty to a tourist, but to me, they provided perfect elevated rooms that potentially hid snipers.

I had personally selected the men for this mission. Two on the first floor and two more shooters hiding in an alley across the street.

Intel provided by the Interpol agents I answered to was that the convoy they were expecting was loaded down with 44-gallon drums of ecstasy tablets. All bound for the US and England. They were to be loaded into shipping containers and then onto ships owned by Gregor Halstett.

The businessman had made his fortune as a drug pusher early in the days. From seller, he became a manufacturer. But he had to rely on others for transport. So, Halstett had cut out the middleman. He'd purchased trucks, which were sufficient for a while, then once he was too big for that, he'd bought a shipping line.

Drugs were very lucrative indeed. Especially when your income was somewhere north of a billion dollars a year from the sale of illegal pills.

Because of my experience, I had been approached by Interpol to see if I would be willing to head up a taskforce to take Halstett's operation off the map. Tonight was part of that operation. Two-hundred million dollars' worth of pills was about to go out. The convoy was under armed escort. What drug kingpin worth his salt wouldn't have his own small army?

"Eagle One, we have vehicles approaching from the west." The voice was British, a female. Her name was Lisa Geddes. In the past, she had been flying UAVs for the MOD, or Ministry of Defense. Now she did it for Interpol. "Four trucks and four escort vehicles."

"Copy," I said over my comms. "Eagles Three and Five, stand by. Take out the driver in the lead vehicle and the one in the rear. Then pick your targets from there. I want the street blocked."

"Copy."

"What are you doing, John?" a new voice asked.

"What you hired me to do, Giselle."

"I hired you to stop a kingpin, not start a war."

"There'll be no war. Just a little scuffle."

"Two mikes," Lisa said, cutting across their conversation.

"Get ready, Two, and Four."

I drew my SIG Sauer P226. If things went as I hoped

they would, I wouldn't even have to fire it. Headlights appeared around the corner and the vehicles started toward our positions.

"On my mark."

I waited.

The vehicles drew closer.

I waited longer.

"One, intel has Halstett with the convoy."

I was hoping the intel was gold. What better way to finish off the night?

My face grew grim. "Three, two, one…execute."

My target, Halstett, had been watching the streetlamps slide by as his SUV led the way through the Antwerp streets. Normally he wouldn't come with a shipment, but tonight was different. The fifty-two-year-old balding entrepreneur wanted to make sure that the shipment arrived on time and intact. He had received word that Interpol was closing in on his operation, so he decided this was to be the last for a few months. It was getting too hot, and he needed things to cool before starting again.

There were four trucks. Three were loaded with drugs, the fourth was filled with his men, his quick reaction force. The Mexican cartels were not the only ones who could raise their own army at a moment's notice.

He had the same resources.

"Are there any problems, Jan?" Halstett asked the man in the front passenger seat.

"None so far, Mr. Halstett."

The kingpin nodded. Another fifteen minutes and they would be at the port.

They rounded the corner and the driver sped up once

more, approaching an intersection ahead. Halstett looked out the window as the buildings flicked by.

Something moved to his right, a figure in a doorway. He frowned and was about to speak to Jan when the windscreen popped, and the driver jerked violently as a bullet punched into his face. His foot reflexively trod forcefully on the gas pedal, and the vehicle sped up and pulled to the right.

Even as it was happening, Jan was calling out a warning over his comms. They were being ambushed, but the question was, by whom?

The lead SUV swerved to the right and crashed into the wall of the building across the street. I looked to the rear of the convoy and saw that the last one had smashed into the rear of the one directly in front of it.

The snipers fired three more shots between them, their targets were the drivers of the trucks and SUVs. Without them, they were going nowhere.

Emanating from the convoy were shouts, and I suddenly had a bad thought. One which came to fruition when the last truck disgorged its load of men from the rear. Heavily armed men.

"Two and Four. Last truck in line. Hammer them."

The two Interpol special operators opened fire, showing Halstett's men no mercy. I muttered a curse. This was all wrong. They had to have known, hence the extra security. "They knew," I said into my comms. "They fucking well knew."

"How could they?" Giselle snapped as I opened fire with my SIG.

"Not in my neighborhood," I replied. "But if you don't get some help out here for us, we're fucked."

A shooter opened fire at me with an automatic weapon. I turned to meet the threat as bullets hammered into the sandstone wall beside me, leaving scars in the soft rock.

The gunfire had come from the lead SUV. I opened fire but missed as the man ducked around to the opposite side. He went to the rear, and I saw him helping someone out of the back seat.

Halstett!

I fired off five shots in the retreating men's direction as they ran into the alley. "I have eyes on Halstett."

"Don't let him get away, John," Giselle said.

"Eagle Two, take over. Keep them pinned down until help arrives."

"Copy, One."

I ran across the street toward the damaged SUV. Off to my left, a figure materialized. I fired twice, and the figure disappeared.

Slipping around the rear of the smashed SUV, I kept running after the retreating figures in the alley.

The bigger one, obviously Halstett's bodyguard, turned and opened fire with his weapon. Bullets sliced through the air, forcing me to take cover. I dived behind an industrial dumpster as bullets spanged off it.

I waited for the shooting to stop and emerged from cover to see them disappearing around the corner of the alley mouth at the far end.

"Lisa, do you have eyes on the target?"

"Copy."

"Don't lose them."

I began running again, and when I reached the end of the alley, I turned left to see the targets further along the street, passing under a streetlamp. "Giselle, make sure my people stay out of trouble."

"I'm in constant contact with them, John. If it gets bad, I'll pull them out."

I ran along the sidewalk, my P226 in hand. Lisa's voice sounded in my ear. "John, they turned into another alley about fifty meters ahead across the street."

"Copy," I panted.

I started across the street and stopped suddenly as a vehicle appeared and almost ran me down. Pausing until it passed, I made another attempt to get across.

Entering the alley mouth, I stopped dead. The darkness was stygian. So much darker than the last one and I was unable to see a thing. They could be anywhere, just waiting.

"Lisa, did they come out the other end?"

"I'm not sure. I don't—"

Gunfire sprayed the alley mouth, forcing me to drop to the damp asphalt. "Shit. There's your fucking answer."

I fired three shots, hoping it would give me time to back up and take cover behind the corner of the building.

"Targets going up, John," Lisa said.

I peered around the corner and could see the outline of a fire escape. Even though I couldn't see those I was chasing, it was the only place they could be. However, this gave the shooter the high ground and put me at a disadvantage. "Lisa, I need another way."

"Further along the street, John, there is another alley. I can make out the fire escape on ISR. It's the only way they can go unless they head inside the building."

"Copy," I replied and began running once more.

Reaching the alley, I swung into it, then ran along until I stood under the fire escape. The bottom rung on the ladder was too high and I couldn't reach it. Looking around, I saw a dumpster. I hurried over to it and began to wheel it into place under the ladder.

I climbed onto it and started my ascent. When I reached the rooftop, I crouched and paused. "Lisa, where are they?"

"Halfway across, you'll see some air conditioning towers. They're there."

"Thanks."

Crouching low, I started across the rooftop, trying to keep to the shadows.

"John, they're about twenty meters ahead of you."

I didn't answer.

A gun shot sounded and I threw myself sideways, or I would have been killed. Bullets cracked close and I returned fire. That elicited a cry of pain, and the shooting stopped. I moved forward, the P226 raised to fire.

I found Halstett's man hunched over and bleeding. He reached for his fallen weapon, but I kicked him in the head, knocking him out cold.

"Lisa, I need a fix on—"

"Drop your weapon."

"Don't bother, I found him." I turned and saw the man I'd been hunting pointing a Glock in my direction. "Thanks for not running away. I'm getting too old to be chasing people across rooftops."

He smiled wickedly. "Your chasing days are done, my friend," Halstett replied.

"Yeah, I'm starting to get too old for this shit. It's better this way."

"What way?"

"Me killing you here."

Halstett frowned and then laughed.

I shot him.

Charles German gave me a disproving look. "You killed him in cold blood?"

"I neutralized a threat."

"What next?"

It was called Molly's Irish Pub, which served great beer. I sat at a table on my own, drinking from a bottle. The beer was cold, and condensation had formed on the brown glass of the bottle and ran down the side in rivulets. I took a sip and placed it on the table. Over in the corner, a group of men and women cheered as they watched the rugby on a large screen. Ireland was playing Wales.

I was on my second when the woman sat down. She had short blonde hair, a small, pointed nose, and wore a long black coat over her clothing. She placed a Guinness on the table and said, "Hello, Mr. Kane."

"Was this the first time you met Holly Smith?" German interrupted again.

"Yes. I'd never seen her before."

"What next?"

I stared at her and said, "Do I know you? Wait, MI6, right?"

"I guess I could be mistaken for that. You are partially right. I am British Intelligence. But we'll leave it at that. My name is Holly Smith."

"What can I do for you, Holly Smith?"

"I would like you to come and work for British Intelligence."

"Doing what?"

"Investigating an incident in Syria. A gas attack on a village."

"And?"

"I'll tell you more if you decide to come in." Holly handed me a card. "If you decide to, I'll expect you here in a couple of days."

"Chandler House?"

"Yes." Holly got to her feet. "Good evening."

And just like that, she was gone. Short, swift, and leaving an everlasting impression.

"Where does Mr. Jensen come into the story?" Christine Ryan asked.

"I'm just getting to that."

CITY SQUARE, LEEDS

That was my first introduction to Holly Smith, but she wasn't done yet. She had another target in her sights.

It was called a square but was technically a triangle. Six roads met here, including Park Row, Infirmary, and Quebec. Watching over it all was a large statue of the Black Prince, Edward. Except, at this point in time, he had help. One Raymond *Knocker* Jensen.

He scratched his beard while eyes searched around the crowd. Somewhere among them was Michael O'Rourke. Leader of the Populist Front of the New IRA. Or whatever they were calling themselves.

Intel had them making some kind of strike. Whether it was a bomb or something else, they couldn't be sure. But it would be something.

"Raymond, talk to me," Peters said in his ear.

Brown eyes flicked through the crowd, and the former SAS operator was conscious of the pressure at the base of his spine from the SIG Sauer P226.

Simon Peters was his operations manager. Head of Team Clover, put together to stop the terrorist threat.

"I've got noth—" He stopped and stared at the mustached man near the statue of the Black Prince. "Hold it, boss, I might have something. Zoom in on the X-Ray with the mustache near Eddie."

Watching the man, he had a reasonable idea who it was but wanted confirmation. Moments later, Peters said, "Confirm Craig Murphy."

"O'Rourke can't be far away," Knocker said. "Everyone, keep your eyes open."

Knocker kept his gaze on Murphy. "One, I have another X-Ray at the restaurant. Seated outside."

"Keep an eye on him, Three."

"One, tick off another X-Ray near the yellow phone box."

"Copy, Two," Knocker replied.

"One, I just had an X-Ray put something in a trash can near the traffic lights."

"Could you tell what it was, Four?" Knocker asked, his heartbeat quickening.

"Negative. Maybe a backpack, but I can't be positive."

"Boss?"

"Wait."

"Boss, if that was a bomb, we need to clear the square."

"I agree, but if we do that, we tip off O'Rourke. Hold position."

Knocker became anxious. "You want to sacrifice innocents, boss? That's what you'll be doing if we don't move."

There was silence on the other end of the comms. Then, "All right, Jensen, have one of your people check it out. Discreetly."

"Roger that. Two, you're closest, do it."

"Copy."

Knocker watched his second-in-command move toward the trash can. As he did, he picked up a piece of paper to use as cover. A man putting refuse in the bin.

Turning his gaze back to the statue of Edward, Knocker saw that Murphy was gone. "Shit. Murphy is on the move. Does anyone have eyes on him?"

"I have him walking toward the restaurant."

Knocker looked and saw him. The roar of a bus drew his attention as it pulled away from the bus stop. "One, we have a problem."

Knocker turned to where Two stood by the trash can. "Go ahead."

"I've not got x-ray vision, but I'd say we've got a bomb here."

"Get rid of—"

BOOM!

The bomb exploded, enveloping the agent beside it. Shrapnel was flung across the square, tearing through the citizens who were there. Limbs were severed, other ghastly wounds were caused, and panic was almost immediate.

"What happened?" Peters demanded. "I've lost visual. Talk to me, Jensen."

"The fucking bomb went off."

People were running everywhere when sudden gunfire erupted. Knocker's hand immediately went to his P226. "Shots fired! Shots fired!"

Knocker looked for shooters but couldn't see any through the throng. "Anyone got eyes on the shooters?"

"There's one at the restaurant," a voice said. Was it Two or Four?

Knocker pushed through the crowd. "Move. Get out of here."

Then he saw the first shooter. He brought up his handgun to fire, but someone ran in front of him. "Christ. What the hell is going on?"

"They're shooting civilians."

"Put them down."

"I have Murphy, I say again, I have Murphy."

"Where?" Knocker snapped.

"He's moving toward the restaurant."

Knocker looked around and saw him. "I have him."

The Brit ran toward the Irishman's position. "Hey, Murphy, you black-hearted bastard!"

The Irishman turned and saw Knocker standing there. He brought up his gun and opened fire at Knocker, sending him diving to the ground. Cursing, Knocker came up onto a knee and returned fire with his P226. The shots missed, but Murphy dropped the backpack he was carrying and ran.

Knocker knew he should be chasing the terrorist, but

something told him to check the backpack. Especially since the last one had contained a bomb.

He kneeled beside it and unzipped the top, looking within, his worst fears realized. Explosives, wires, and a digital timer counting down. It had one minute left on it. "Bollocks."

Glancing around the immediate area, he saw that there were far too many civilians here and gunfire still rang out. "Peters?"

"I'm here, Jensen."

"I've got a second bomb. It's on a timer."

His fingers flicked over the wires.

"How long?"

"Forty seconds."

"No, no, no. That's not enough time. Can you disarm it?"

"Sure, I can also walk on water."

"Raymond."

"Just shut up, I'm thinking."

Knocker looked at the timer, then the wires, and the wires again. All the time the timer was running down. He was about to die, and he needed a Hail Mary. He grabbed a wire.

"Fucking Irish bastard."

He closed his eyes and pulled.

Nothing happened.

"Hold it," said Jack Holland. "You just pulled the wire and hoped for the best?"

Knocker nodded. "Sure. I had nothing to lose."

"But you did. Did you screw up?"

Knocker shrugged. "No. We missed a bomb."

Knocker looked down and saw the timer had stopped on three seconds. He raised his eyebrows. "Bollocks."

"Jensen, what happened?" Peters demanded.

"It's fine. It didn't—"

BOOM!

Knocker's ears were ringing as he climbed out of the darkness. He coughed and could feel blood as it ran down the side of his face. In the distance, he could hear Peters shouting at him. "Jensen, what happened? Talk to me, damn it. Was that another bomb?"

Pushing himself up onto his knees, Knocker looked around. There were even more bodies on the square. It seemed that the second bomb had been bigger. He shook his head as his vision blurred and then cleared. Standing there, looking down at him, was a man wearing a suit, covered in blood, missing an arm.

"Shit. Sit down, mate. You have to sit down."

He just stared at the Brit.

Knocker tried to stand up and fell back to his knees. His world spun and he tried to shake it loose. Eventually, he came to his feet, but the armless man had moved on. The Brit said, "Does anyone have eyes on Murphy?"

"No—wait. He's headed up Quebec Street."

Gathering all his strength and his sidearm, Knocker managed to get to his feet. Around him was utter chaos. He started toward Quebec when a shooter appeared in front of him. Knocker brought up the P226 and fired three rounds into the man, killing him outright.

The former SAS operator's shuffle became a walk, became a jog as he headed to Quebec Street. "This is Jensen, I'm going after Murphy."

The street was narrow and full of civilians trying to escape the carnage of Leeds Square. People screamed in panic and vehicles were abandoned in the middle of the thoroughfare. Orange bollards were on the sidewalk where workmen had been not long before, scared away by the explosions and the gunfire.

Knocker's eyes darted left and right as he tried to find his target. "Peters, do you see him?"

"No, not yet—wait. Ahead of you in a blue shirt, green cap."

Then Knocker saw him. "Got him."

He gave chase, and just as he was closing the distance, Murphy turned hard left and disappeared through a red door.

"What the hell? Peters, did you see that?"

"Yes."

"Where does it go?"

"Not sure."

"Well, bloody find out."

"Wait, one." There was a moment's silence, then, "The tunnels. It goes down to the tunnels."

"What tunnels?"

"They're leftovers from World War Two. The place is riddled with them."

"Copy."

Knocker went through the doorway and saw the steps leading down and away from him. He reached into his pocket and pulled out a small penlight, switching it on. "Talk to me."

A new voice filled his ear. "Raymond, do you hear me?"

"I've got you, Becca."

"OK, listen closely. You've got stairs in front of you."

"Yes."

"Go down and turn right."

Knocker started down. "Why right?"

"Because that is the only way out."

He reached the bottom of the stairs and turned into a long tunnel. He stopped and listened and could hear footsteps receding into the distance. "I can hear him."

As he started along the tunnel, lights flickered on. Becca asked, "Is that better?"

The sudden brightness made him pause. All along the ceiling was a long tube of conduit, with lights in cage covers every forty or so feet. "It's good to be able to see properly."

"Good. Now, up ahead, there is a junction. Three ways. You'll have to try and figure out which way he's gone."

"Copy."

When Knocker reached the junction, he paused. His ears strained to hear anything that might tell him the way Murphy had gone. Then he heard the echoes. The only problem was he couldn't tell if they came from ahead of him or to the left.

"Heads or tails, Knocker old mate? I know, tails. Left it is."

The former SAS man sped up, trying not to fall too far behind—if he was indeed on the right track.

The tunnels were constructed of brick and concrete, and every now and then, there was a memorial plaque on the wall commemorating different nights of the blitz.

"Raymond, up ahead and around the corner, there is another junction. One path leads up some steps to another door like the one you—"

CLANG!

"He's gone out the door," Knocker said, starting to run.

He took the stairs two at a time and burst out onto the street, almost knocking a pedestrian over. He looked left and right but saw nothing. "Where is he?"

No answer.

"Someone tell me where the fuck Murphy is."

"We don't know," Peters responded. "We don't have him on ISR."

"Fuck!"

———

"I have him!"

"Where?" Knocker demanded.

"Headed east away from you," Becca said hurriedly.

Knocker turned his head and saw the man he was looking for in the distance. "Got the bastard."

He started running once more after the Irishman. The distance closed rapidly, and once Knocker deemed himself close enough, he brought up his weapon and said, "That's far enough, Murphy."

The Irishman stopped and turned slowly. There was a weird smile on his face, and he slowly opened his jacket to reveal a suicide vest. "I do believe you have a problem."

"No problem, Paddy, I'll just put a bullet in your fucking head and take my chances."

Murphy showed Knocker the trigger in his right hand. Knocker stared at it and frowned. The Irishman said, "Do you think—"

Knocker fired.

The trigger fell from Murphy's hand, hitting the side-walk alongside his finger. Knocker said, "You'd think even a fucking Paddy like you would know the difference between a dead-man switch and a straightforward trigger."

The shocked expression was still etched deeply on the Irishman's face when Knocker shot him in the head. "This is Jensen. Target down. Send bomb techs. We've got a suicide vest. Out."

Knocker looked at the dead man once more and sat down on the sidewalk. "What a fucked up day."

The medic gave Knocker the once over to check that he was in one piece. His hearing was still a little muddled and he felt like he'd gone twelve rounds in a heavy-weight battle, but other than that, he was seemingly all right.

"Clean bill of health?"

He looked up at the woman facing him. "What the fuck do you want, Holly?"

Holly Smith smiled at him. "Is that the way to greet an old friend, Raymond?" she asked.

"We're not friends."

"Really? I thought that since we slept together that we would be friends."

Knocker grunted. "We only slept together because you wanted me to do something for you."

"Semantics."

"Yeah, well I don't plan on doing it again."

"I have a job for you. Well, you and your friend, Mr. Kane, actually."

"Doing what?" the former SAS man sighed.

"Investigating a gas attack on a village in Syria. Get in, get evidence, and get out. That's all."

Knocker shook his head. "That's never all."

"I'll see you tomorrow at Chandler House."

"Whatever."

She had her next man.

"So, you knew Holly Smith intimately?" Christine Ryan asked.

"Yeah, I screwed her."

Ryan glared at him. "You are an animal."

"That's the thing with us animals," Knocker said. "We're the ones you all turn to when you want something done."

German cleared his throat. "Continue, gentlemen."

CHAPTER 2

Chandler House looked a lot like Bletchley Park of World War Two fame from the outside. But on the inside, it was more modern. I was shown through to a waiting area, where I was offered a mug of coffee to ease the length of the wait.

Moments after my arrival, a familiar face was shown through the door. I said, "What are you doing here?"

"Apparently, babysitting you," Knocker replied. He sat down next to me on a hard plastic seat. "You'd think that British Intelligence would have better seats."

"Getting soft?"

"Not likely."

"You look like shit, by the way."

"What do you expect? I got blown the fuck up."

"That'll do it. What did they tell you?"

"Something about Syria."

I nodded.

We sat in silence for the next thirty minutes, Knocker lightly sleeping. Minute thirty-one saw the emergence of Holly Smith. I nudged my friend. Holly was wearing a dark pants suit with a bulge under the left arm where her weapon was holstered. "Come with me, lads."

We followed her along a hallway and up a narrow flight of stairs. When we reached the landing, turning left, we walked along to the office at the end of the hallway. There was a small sign on the door which said, Middle East Branch.

Inside, the office was a well-lit room with white wainscoting, the walls above covered in patterned wallpaper. To break it up, there were a couple of paintings and etchings. In the center of the room was a large dark wood desk with a middle-aged man seated behind it. Knocker took one look at him and muttered a curse under his breath.

"Good to see you, Jensen," the man greeted him. "You wouldn't have been my first pick either, but Holly insisted that you pair came as a team."

"Another person you've made a lasting impression on in your short, chaotic life?" I asked, raising an eyebrow and smirking at Knocker.

"Typical fucking head shed," Knocker replied.

"I can send you back, you know, Jensen," the man said.

"Yes, sir," the former SAS man replied, sounding like he was spitting out a bitter pill.

"What was your problem with Mr. Short?" Holland asked.

"He hated me, and I didn't like him," Knocker replied. "Now will you stop asking so many damn questions and let us tell the bloody story?"

Holland nodded. "Of course."

The man's eyes switched to me. "Mr. Kane, I'm Brian Short, head of the Middle East Branch here at British Intelligence."

"Mr. Short," I said with a nod.

"You were chosen because we need someone to go into Syria. You and Jensen have a reputation of getting things done."

"Depends on what things you want to get done," I replied.

"We want you to slip into Syria from Turkey and have a look at a Kurdish village that was supposedly gassed. Nothing too stressful. In and out. Get whatever evidence you can."

I nodded.

"Holly will brief you. Good luck."

With that, the meeting was over, and we followed Holly from the room.

Holly took us into a smaller office and we were each given a folder. Knocker glared at her and said, "You could have mentioned that bastard was here."

She shrugged. "It must have slipped my mind. Is it going to be a problem, Raymond?"

"Just as long as he stays out of my way."

"Read me in, buddy," I said.

"He was military intelligence in Afghanistan. Sent my team into a zone supposedly clean. All we were to do was see if we could find caches of weapons. Except the damn place was loaded with Taliban. He put us in as bait for a rapid response force of paras. The Tallies waited until we were smack in the center of their trap before slamming the door shut. I lost three men in the first few minutes. A fourth before the paras arrived. By the time we were out of the danger zone, every man, including myself, had been wounded in some way. Whatever you do, Reaper, don't trust the bastard."

"You won't have to," Holly said. "Trust me. I'm your handler for this mission. Shall we get started?"

Knocker grunted. "Why ever not?"

"You'll see on the map within the folder there is a small

village marked inside a red circle. We received intel that it was attacked from the air using gas. We're not sure why or if the reports are true. We want you to go and have a look."

"Who supposedly did it?" I asked.

"Not sure. Syrians or Russians, take your pick."

Chemical weapons had already been used inside Syria. The civil war had seen Sarin used multiple times. One of the worst was in Khan Shaykhun, where up to one hundred-plus people were killed and around three hundred affected. The Syrians denied the attack, while the Russians said that it was staged. However, it wasn't enough to stop the US from striking back, and over fifty cruise missiles rained down on the airfield that had been the launching point for the attack.

"Was it Sarin?" Knocker asked.

"We're not sure. All reports indicate that it could have been something new."

"That's still the wild west," I pointed out. "Turkey and the Kurds are still at war. Is there anything to indicate it might have been them?"

"If there was, we wouldn't need you."

"What backup do we have?" Knocker asked.

"Very little. Your contact in Turkey will be a woman named Amira. She is a Kurd. She will get you into Syria and guide you to where you need to go. If you need help, there are some friendly Kurdish forces she will introduce you to."

"What about weapons?" I asked.

"You'll get them before you leave Turkey," Holly replied as she picked up her folder.

"Where do we meet our contact?" Knocker asked Holly.

"Kayseri. She will contact you at your hotel."

"When do we leave?" I asked.

"Tonight. Everything is ready."

I nodded. "No time like the present."

Knocker nodded as well.

"By the way," I said, "tell me who you've pissed off in Turkey, Knocker."

The former SAS man paused and then shook his head. "You don't want to know."

"You're right. It's probably best."

Christine Ryan looked at the open folder in front of her. "You seem to piss people off wherever you go."

Knocker grinned at her. "It's one of my many talents."

KAYSERI, TURKEY

We got off the plane in Kayseri and caught a taxi into the city to our hotel. It was the first time either of us had been to the city, and we had to admit it wasn't at all what we'd expected.

The taxi dropped us outside the hotel, and I paid the fare. We went inside, the bellhop following us with our bags. All two of them.

Inside, the foyer was large with polished granite floors. In various corners, there were palms in pots and throughout were pillars made from imported Italian marble.

We checked in and started across to the bank of elevators. Knocker said, "Standing next to the pillar with a newspaper."

I said, "I've got him."

"Makes me feel like I'm in a Cold War movie."

"There's another sitting on the lounge across the foyer," I said.

"Bloody Russians. Hopeless."

"How do you know they're Russian?" I asked.

"I can smell the bastard from here."

We reached the elevators with the bellhop close behind.

He escorted us to our room, and I slipped him a couple of dollars to go away. Knocker turned to me. "What now?"

"We wait."

Five minutes later, there was a knock on the door and a voice said, "Housekeeping."

Knocker looked at me. I walked over to the door and said, "We didn't order any."

"Yes, you did, sir."

Looking out through the peephole in the door, I saw a woman standing next to a trolley filled with linen and toiletries. "Amira?"

"Open the door."

I did as requested, stepping back to admit the woman. She was undoubtedly Middle Eastern, and her hair was long and tied back. Her eyes matched her hair and gave her almost flawless face a sultry look. She pushed the trolley in, and he closed the door behind her.

"You are late," Amira said.

"We got caught collecting our baggage," I replied.

Reaching down into the trolley, she moved a sheet around. Finding what she was seeking, she straightened and passed each of us matching handguns. Glock 45s.

"Take these. You must be careful. The foyer is full of Russian agents."

"Why?" Knocker asked.

"They look for targets who might be crossing the border to help the Kurds and the rebels."

"So, people like us," I replied.

She stared at me with sultry eyes. "Yes, people like you."

Amira handed us spare magazines of ammunition, and we sequestered them where we could access them quickly if we needed to. I looked at her and said, "Thank you."

"I will be back tomorrow. We will leave then. If you have any problems, you can call this number. Only once, after that, it will automatically disconnect so no one can trace it."

I nodded.

Then she left.

Unknown to us both, in a building nearby, our Russian friends were having a meeting. The agents were from the SVR, who reported directly to the Russian president. What they were doing in Kayseri, I had no idea, but they wanted me and Knocker.

"We are under orders to catch or kill both of these men," Igor Ionov told his men. "Either way, it will not matter."

"What about the people in the hotel?" a younger man asked his gray-haired commander. "The security."

"Use your discretion until you can't. There will be eight of you. More than enough to succeed in your mission."

"Comrade?"

Igor turned to stare at another of his men. This one was older than the others. A team leader. "What is it, Roman?"

"I have looked into both of these men. They are very accomplished. I have a feeling that this will not be as simple as predicted."

"Do you want more men?"

"Do you have any?"

Igor nodded. "There is a team of SOF not far from here. I can have them standby."

"I think it would be best," Roman said. "Under no circumstances must these men be underestimated."

Apparently, our reputation had preceded us. I don't know how they knew we were there, but as the British would say, they were about to throw the kitchen sink at us.

It started with a knock on the door and a woman on the other side announcing, "Room service."

She might as well have been waving a red fucking flag. I mean, it was nine at night. I looked at Knocker, who already had his Glock in hand. He stared at me and brought his finger to his lips. Like a cat, he moved toward the door. He looked through the peep hole and saw a woman on the other side dressed in black. Her eyes shifted to the right. She was looking at someone.

Using hand signals, my friend indicated that there were at least two in the hallway. I took out my own Glock and turned, diverting my gaze to the sliding doors that led onto the balcony. There was movement out there as well.

"Get down!" I shouted and threw myself to the floor behind the sofa.

The glass exploded inwardly at the same time as the door into our suite was breached. It blew off its hinges and skidded across the tile floor. Knocker had thrown himself through the open doorway into the bathroom.

Using the sofa for cover, I opened fire at the armed figures coming into the room via the balcony. I saw one fall while a second staggered. Something bounced off the hard floor and exploded. The stun grenade was shattering. I felt myself falling sideways, half-blinded, ears ringing.

The Glock fell from my grasp onto the cold floor. Meanwhile, Knocker had shot the first breacher through the door but had also succumbed to the stun grenade. Soon we were both face down and had our hands tied, bags over our heads. Voices—Russian—sounded as though they were miles away.

"How did you know they were Russian?"

I glared at German. It was a stupid question and it pissed me off. So, I ignored it.

We were both roughly dragged to our feet and dragged —carried toward the door.

Somewhere along the way I had blacked out. When I became aware of my surroundings once more, we were both lying down as a vehicle, a transit van, bumped along the streets at a solid pace.

I heard a siren as an emergency response vehicle went past. My body lurched as the van hit a hole in the street. It hurt. The voices sounded clearer now. One of the Russians was saying that they should have killed us, while another stated that their handler wanted us alive if possible.

The woman said something I didn't quite make out. But fifteen minutes or so later, the van made a hard turn right, rocked violently, and stopped.

I could hear a chain rattling in the distance. Someone was lowering a roller door. Maybe we were in a warehouse.

I do know that we were dragged from the van and dumped onto a cold concrete floor.

"Easy, fuck you," I heard Knocker say.

Our hoods were ripped from our heads, and I found that I was right. We were in a substantial warehouse. The roof was high over our heads, steel girders looked to be rusted as they were partially hidden behind the large lights.

I blinked my eyes a few times and focused on our captors. All, except for two men, wore ski masks.

"Pick them up," a gray-haired man with a lined face ordered.

Moments later, we were hauled up and placed on two chairs, where we were fixed by ropes. The man who gave the orders moved in closer to us. "Mr. Kane, Mr. Jensen."

"The prick knows us, Reaper," Knocker said to me.

"It would seem so."

"Your reputation precedes you."

"No good having a reputation if everyone wants to kill you," I replied. "Who the fuck are you?"

"My name is Igor."

Knocker chuckled. "Sounds like some fuck from the Addams family or fucking Transylvania."

Igor nodded at one of his men who stepped forward and slapped Knocker across the face, drawing blood.

"Jesus bollocks," he grunted, spitting on the floor. "What the fuck was that for?"

"Respect, Mr. Jensen. Now, I would like for you, one of you, to answer my questions."

I stared at him.

"Now, what are you doing here?"

There was no point in not answering, so I did. "Working for UNICEF."

Then one of his people hit me.

In the mouth.

Drawing blood.

I spat on the floor.

Now we were both bleeding.

"Shall we try again?"

Knocker said, "All right, I'll tell you. We're looking for your wife so we can take turns with her. Apparently, she sucks good cock."

"That's not nice, Raymond," I said in a reprimanding tone. "Have some respect for the man from the SVR."

Knocker raised his eyebrows. "SVR?"

"That's right."

"What the fuck are the SVR doing here?"

"I don't know. Let's ask. What the fuck are you doing here, Igor?"

"Didn't you know? Turkey is the new playground for spies. Now, what are you doing here?"

"Looking for you," I replied.

He stared at me, not knowing if I was serious or yanking his chain. He made his decision and said, "Get it."

Knocker looked at me. "Get what?"

"I don't know."

"Get what, Igor?"

"It is a surprise."

"I don't like surprises."

"You'll like this one," he assured Knocker. "It will make you…jump."

"Shit. He's smiling, Reaper. I hate it when the bad guys fucking smile. No good can ever come from it."

Then I saw what they were wheeling in on a trolley. Knocker was right.

CHAPTER 3

Have you ever been happy when someone else is being tortured instead of you? Well, while my British friend was shouting his lungs out, electricity coursing through his body, I was feeling quite relieved that it was him and not me.

They'd been at it for five minutes, although that felt closer to an hour. I'm guessing to Knocker, it seemed like a lifetime.

The leads were pulled away from his heaving body and he went limp. Looking up at his torturer, he hissed, "Fuck you."

I had to give it to him, he was tough. But more than that, he was mad. Igor looked at me and said, "You can stop this by telling me why you are here."

I looked at Knocker, whose chest was heaving.

"Don't bloody tell him, Reaper. I can take whatever they've got."

The leads touched bare skin and my friend started to shout again.

"All right, stop."

The torturer halted his ministrations and stood back. He

looked at Igor, who nodded and said, "Very well, Mr. Kane, I am waiting."

"We are going into Syria."

"Why?"

"We've been hired to find Jim James."

"Jim James?"

I nodded. "That's right. Find him."

Jim James was a home-grown terrorist who came to Syria to join IS. With their so-called defeat, the man known as Hacksaw Jim, because of the way he liked to execute hostages, had never been found. Not publicly.

In fact, he'd been picked up by an SBS team in a raid on the Somali coast. Somehow, he'd made his way there. Now he was tucked away in a dark hole on the island of Gibraltar. But these guys didn't know that.

"I think you are lying," Ionov, so I found out his name to be, said to me.

Then he turned the charge up, and Knocker screamed louder, his teeth gnashing together, his jaw set tight.

"It's true," I shouted above the chilling sound.

The electricity ceased and I heard my friend say, "Ah, bollocks, I pissed myself."

"Are you going to tell me the truth now, Mr. Kane?"

"Yes—"

Suddenly, the room erupted in gunfire. The SVR agents tried to respond to the sudden attack, but the surprise was too great. Among the chaos, I remember seeing Ionov disappearing through a door like a rat abandoning a sinking ship.

"You let him get away," Christine Ryan said with a confused expression on her face.

"Yeah, I was going to jump up, chair and all, and chase after him."

"Continue, Mr. Kane," Holland said.

Then came the silence, the eerie type that usually follows

the sound of savage battle. I took stock of myself, feeling relieved that I hadn't been shot in the chaos. The question was, who were these masked figures I was now staring at?

The answer was provided to me when one of them stepped forward and removed said mask. Amira smiled at me. "I leave you alone for five minutes and this is what happens."

"How about you set me free?" I asked her.

Moments later, we were both liberated from our restraints. Knocker looked down at himself and said to Amira, "I don't suppose you have a clean pair of pants?"

She pointed at the dead SVR agents. "Take your pick."

"Great, I'll be wearing dead man's pants."

"We need to get out of here before the police come."

Meanwhile, Knocker had found a pair of pants that would suffice. He looked down and saw his ankles showing to the world. "Just great. My shoes need to have a party and invite my pants down."

We exited the building and climbed into a dark green SUV. We drove away just as the first police cars started to arrive.

"Who were they?" Amira asked me.

"Inquisitive SVR agents. The one who got away called himself—"

"Igor Ionov," Amira finished for me. "He is a dangerous man. He has people in the government that his money has bought."

"Not a nice guy," I replied.

"We will take you somewhere safe until it is time to cross the border," Amira told me.

Knowing that the hotel was out, I said, "Sounds good."

We spent the remainder of the night driving toward Gaziantep. At one stage, we were stopped at a checkpoint where we used our fake credentials as reporters to pass through. From there, we kept driving until we reached the city.

We were sequestered inside a small home constructed of red mudbrick on the outskirts of the city. Amira had changed from her jeans to more favorable camouflage pants, which, I must say, hugged her ass in all the right places.

I was drinking a cup of bitter coffee when she found me by myself in the backyard which was surrounded by a high mudbrick wall.

"You need to get some rest," she told me. "We will cross over into Syria tonight."

She confused me, so I asked, "Why are you here?"

"I am Kurdish."

She said it as though the explanation would be enough. I nodded and left it at that. Instead, I asked, "Do you get people across the border often?"

She nodded. "Some."

"Agents?"

"All kinds. People like you, mercenaries, some others who sell weapons."

"So you work for the highest bidder?" I asked her.

Amira shook her head. "No, I have rules."

I stared into her round, dark eyes. "What rules?"

"Like not sleeping with customers."

With a nod, I said, "Good rule to have."

"I thought so."

"What if I fire you."

She grinned. "Then you will have no one to get you over the border."

I returned her smile with one of my own. "Touché."

One of Amira's men appeared. He spoke to her briefly,

and she looked at me. "Our transport has arrived for tonight. Would you care to inspect it?"

Following her out the front, we found a MAN truck. It was loaded with bags of something, possibly wheat. It was white and looked like it had seen better days. Amira said, "We will use it to get across the border. In the back is a compartment big enough for four people to hide with packs and weapons which are already there."

Knocker appeared. "Are you sure it won't chuck a shit and fall apart?"

"Would you like us to try to get a nice shiny truck across the border?"

My friend shrugged. "Just asking."

I looked it over and checked the compartment. Amira said, "Your MI6 supplied the weapons and equipment."

I looked it over. There were two new AK-12s as well as MP-446 Viking handguns. All Russian weapons. Someone had also thrown in body armor and binoculars, along with spare ammunition and some grenades.

"No NVGs," Knocker said to me.

"Can't have everything, I guess."

Satisfied with what we'd been supplied from MI6, we went back inside. By this time, my friend had found pants that actually fit him. Something I was pleased with because his constant complaints were starting to irritate me.

Then we waited.

We left after dark to cover the hundred-plus kilometers to the border crossing. We were secured away in the rear compartment. Knocker, myself, Amira, and her man Ferhad. It was a rough ride but one that had to be endured if we were to cross into Syria.

Three hours after we left, the truck slowed and stopped

at the border checkpoint. After some to and fro, the border guards walked around the truck checking it. There was banging on the outside, and I heard the tailgate screech as it was opened. Then came the savage barking of the dog stationed purposefully for just the occasion.

Some angry words were passed back to the driver, and I could only guess that the border guard was threatening to shoot the animal. Then, after a brief argument, the tailgate was closed, and we were allowed to pass through the checkpoint.

"The dog, huh?" I said after a while.

"Works all the time," Amira said.

"Don't the border guards get sick of the animal?"

"Of course. They threaten to shoot it every time, but they never do."

We drove ten kilometers before the truck stopped. Once we were let out, we changed into our gear and started our journey once more. Knocker and I loaded our weapons while Amira and her man readied their own. To my surprise, they were armed with AK-74s.

"Can you ride horses?" Amira asked me.

"Not for a long time." I looked at Knocker. "What about you?"

"I can ride a horse like I ride a barstool when I'm as drunk as ten men."

"I have a feeling we're about to put our skills to use."

And we were. For once we had all our equipment off the truck, it drove off, and we were left standing in the middle of nowhere.

My AK-12 snapped around and pointed at the head of the man who walked out of the darkness leading five horses. It was an hour before dawn, and we'd been holding in place for four hours. It was typical nighttime weather. Cold.

Without lowering my weapon, I asked, "Are we waiting for him?"

Amira stepped forward and spoke hurriedly. Then she turned to me and said, "Lower your weapon."

I lowered the AK-12 and waited to see what would happen next. Amira turned to me and said, "Pick yourself a horse. We must leave now. There are Syrian patrols in the area."

A bay with a mean disposition was a poor choice of animal. My thought after it threw me the first time was to put a bullet between its ears. Then I thought, why blame the poor animal? Shoot the son of a bitch who brought it.

We traveled until the sun came up and rested for twenty minutes. Amira walked over to me and said, "How are you feeling?"

"My butt hurts already." And it did.

She grinned. "You will get used to it."

"I hope I do," Knocker said. "My ass feels like it's on fire."

"We shall keep going soon."

I asked her how much further we had to go. She gave me a funny look and said, "Do you not know?"

"They told us that you would have all the information we required."

"Four days."

"Four days riding?" I asked, unsure if I'd heard her right.

Amira nodded. "Yes. But if we run into trouble, it will be longer."

An image came into my head. One of me walking bow-legged for the rest of my life. It wasn't pretty.

So, away we went again. The Syrian Cavalry. We rode for two days and were resting late on the second day when a small Syrian patrol appeared and bivouacked two hundred meters from the wadi we had stopped in.

Using my binoculars, I watched the vehicles stop and the soldiers set up camp. The afternoon was fading fast, and the nightly chill seemed to fall from the sky like a blanket. It wasn't until after night arrived that we heard the first high-pitched scream.

It was so crisp that I grabbed for my AK-12 and crawled up the lip of the wadi to where Knocker watched the Syrian camp. He said, "I can't see, but they've got at least one woman over there."

Amira appeared beside me. "What is happening?"

"Sounds like our friends are having some fun," I replied.

Another scream reached out across the landscape. Amira said, "We have to help her."

I placed a hand upon her arm. "We can't. If we start something now, it could be the end of everything."

"But we can't just let them defile her."

"We've got no choice," Knocker said. "Like Reaper said, if we start something and word gets out, we'll be up to our asses in Syrians. Or worse, Russian Special Forces. No one is supposed to know we're here, remember?"

Amira didn't like it, and the intermittent screams made it worse. If I'd had my way, Knocker and I would have gone over there and killed every one of them. But as they say in the world of special operations, the mission comes first.

CHAPTER 4

THE HARDEST PART CAME THE FOLLOWING MORNING. THE Syrians broke camp in the cool of the red sunrise and disappeared in a cloud of dust. They left behind them what looked to be a pile of rags among the weeds where they had camped.

I called Knocker over and pointed them out to him. He said after studying them, "That isn't a pile of rags, Reaper."

I nodded. "Yeah, I had that feeling myself. Cover my ass."

Making sure everything was clear, I climbed to my feet and started across the open ground between the wadi and the campsite. I had the AK-12 ready to fire but had a feeling I wouldn't need it.

When I reached the site, I found what I expected to find. The Syrians had killed the woman and covered her with the remnants of her clothing. It was not a pretty picture.

I heard Amira gasp. She had followed me, and her wide eyes were fixated on the dead woman. Her eyes blazed and were suddenly focused on me. "I told you we should have helped her. Now she is dead, and it is because of you."

I waited for her anger to subside. She needed someone

to blame, and I was it. Sobeit. However, like I had said the night before, it was all about the mission.

Amira looked at me and realized I'd been waiting for her to finish. "I am sorry. It wasn't your fault."

"Believe me, I wish we could have done more," I replied to her.

"I will have Ferhad stay behind and bury her. He can then catch up."

I nodded. When we returned to the camp, I gave Knocker a knowing look. He muttered a curse and walked toward his horse, and we continued our journey.

Some things I'm willing to let go once. But never twice. In this case, it might have been a weakness because what happened next put the mission at risk. That night, our friends returned to a different camp adjacent to our own.

"Who would have fucking thought it would happen two nights in a row, Reaper?" Knocker said to me in a low voice. "It's a bloody sign."

The scream of another woman reached out to us, calling for us to do something as it had the night before. He knew what I was thinking. "Don't do it, Reaper. It's a bad idea."

"Are you going to stop me?" I asked.

"Fuck no, I'm going with you."

Decision made.

We slid back down the bank of the wadi to where Amira sat, wringing her hands. I said to her, "You and Ferhad stay here. Knocker and I will be right back."

Her head snapped around. "Where are you going?"

"Over there to say hello," Knocker replied. "We won't be long."

"Let me help."

"No, stay here."

"She is a woman. I am a woman."

She was right. If what was happening to her was what I thought, she would need a woman. I said, "Come so far and wait until I call for you."

"But—"

"Or stay here."

"Fine."

We crept through the dark toward the encampment. When we were halfway, I made Amira hunker down and wait. Then we went the rest of the way. We crouched down outside the range of the firelight and studied the Syrians. There were six of them and the woman.

Who was naked.

I leaned in close to my friend's ear. "You take the three on the right. I'll take the ones on the left."

"Copy that."

My AK-12 came up and I sighted on the first of the Syrians. "Now."

The first shot I fired hit the soldier on the furthest left. I then changed my aim and shot the second one. Beside me, Knocker did the same, working from outside in.

My third target was on top of the woman, grunting as he raped her. As soon as he realized something was wrong, his head popped up, presenting me with a perfect target.

The bullet I fired spread his brain across the ground.

With all six targets down, Knocker and I pushed forward into the camp. Once we were sure everyone was dead, I called Amira in to take care of the sobbing woman.

Knocker said to me, "What are we going to do with these scousers?"

"Make it look like rebels did it."

My friend nodded, knowing what I meant. So we went to work with our knives.

"You risked the mission for the sake of one woman and then mutilated the Syrian soldiers with knives?" German said.

"We did what we had to do to remain undetected," I replied.

"If you wanted to do that, you wouldn't have engaged them in the first place."

We kept riding for the next two days, the woman with us, and it was late on the second when the village came into sight.

"That is it," Amira said to me. "This is what we have come for."

When we reached the village of red brick houses, we were greeted by almost no one. Where the village should have been a hive of activity, this one was almost deserted.

"There are very few left," Amira said to me. "The survivors were lucky."

A dog came out of one of the houses and ran over, barking at my horse. The beast pig-rooted and bucked and threw me off. However, I'd been expecting it and landed on my feet.

An old man appeared. His face was weathered and wrinkled, and when he smiled at me, he had an issue with his teeth. He had none. Amira said, "This is Soran. He is an aga."

I nodded to him and held out my hand. He took it in his. Gone was the strength that it had once held, replaced now with gnarled fingers and callouses from years of work.

"Tell him I am pleased to meet him."

Instead, he surprised me by saying. "I am pleased to meet you also."

We laughed together. "Come and rest. Tomorrow, we shall discuss what you have come here to talk about. A meal will be prepared in your honor."

Amira said something to Soran and pointed at the woman who had come with us. He nodded and said, "She will be taken care of."

That night, we ate Dolma and Kofta. It was prepared by Soran's daughter. His wife, we found out later, died in the attack by the Russians.

I'd never dined on such food before, and I found it nice to eat. Once we were finished, he gave us coffee to wash it down.

Later that evening, Amira came to me in my room. I hadn't asked her to, but was glad she did. The night was cold, and the extra body kept me warm.

The next morning, when we awoke, the sun was well above the horizon. Knocker was playing a game with a handful of children as they sat in a circle. He looked up at me and said, "Have a good night, Reaper?"

"I was warm."

"I bet you were."

Amira emerged, her hair down, and in the sunlight, she was even more beautiful than I had already thought. "Come, we have a meeting."

We found Soran with a group of other men. He stood to greet us, and once again, we shook hands. The others stared at us suspiciously, as though we were their enemies. Knocker and I sat while Amira left us.

One of the men stared at me with anger in his eyes and said something I didn't understand. Beside me, Knocker said, "He wants to know if we are here to help them."

I glanced at my friend who shrugged. "They're big on languages in the SAS."

"You are SAS?" Soran asked.

Knocker shook his head. "Not any longer. Now I just go where I'm asked."

"Can you tell us what happened?" I asked.

Soran told us about the plane and about the men who came into the village. "They piled the bodies up and burned them. Even the reporter."

His words gave me pause. "Wait, there was a reporter?"

"Someone forgot to fucking tell us about that," Knocker growled.

I studied their faces, each remained passive.

"What reporter?" Knocker asked.

"A woman," Soran told us. "Her name was Sarah Nash. She was what she called a free person."

"A freelancer?"

"That is it. She came here to do a story on us. About what the Russian mercenaries were doing in the region."

I looked at Knocker, who had a similar expression on his face as I had on mine. I said, "Are you sure they burned her?"

"Yes."

"What was her name again? What did she look like?"

"Her name was Sarah Nash," Soran said. "She was thin and had red hair. Her skin was too fair for the sun."

I saw Knocker's expression change and left it for the moment.

"What were the Russians up to?" I asked Soran.

"What they are up to normally. Killing us by any means necessary. We complained to the UN, but we got nothing."

I nodded. "I will see what I can do."

"Thank you."

We left the meeting, and once we were out of earshot, I looked at Knocker. "Do you figure she was a reporter?"

He shook his head. "Nope, but there's no way to find out."

"But there is now," I said as I stared at the three people before me. "Who was she?"

They looked at each other before Christine Ryan said, "Her name was Sarah Nash."

"And she got sent in on her own and got gassed for her troubles," Knocker growled.

"At least we know what happened to her," German said. "Continue, please."

Soran followed us away from the meeting. He said, "I have something else."

We turned to meet his advance. "What's that?" I asked.

"There is an airfield, maybe a day and a half ride from here. That is where the gas is held."

I nodded. "Give us a moment."

Once more, Knocker and I walked off on our own. "What do you say?"

"If they have gas there, it's a good time to destroy it."

"We'd need something that goes bang."

I turned to Soran. "You wouldn't have any explosives, would you?"

German frowned at us. "You went off mission. You found out what you needed to, and then disobeyed orders."

I shook my head. "No, we found out what happened, but we still had to find out who and why? If we'd have pulled out then, we would have only completed half a mission."

"Then why the explosives?"

"Target of opportunity," Knocker said.

Soran led us, along with Amira, to a hole in the ground under a chicken coop. He moved it aside and lifted the wooden lid beneath it to reveal a cache of weapons and ammunition. Also, inside were some blocks of C4. I raised my eyebrows in surprise. "Detonators?"

"In the goat pen."

At least he had enough sense to keep them separate. "All right, we'll go and have a look at this airfield. What do you know about it?"

Preparing the horses for travel, we loaded food on the one that Ferhan had been riding. He'd stay in the village until we returned. Along with the food, the C4 was loaded onto the spare horse as well. The detonators were put in a pack on

Knocker's horse. With Amira, there would be the three of us.

She appeared with Soran. "You are almost ready?"

I nodded. "Yes."

"Before you go, I wish to show you something."

I nodded and followed him to the far side of the village. There, surrounded by a newly built stone wall, was a graveyard. He said, "There is no one there. Every stone represents someone who died that day. The size of the stone indicates man, woman, or child."

There were a lot more smaller stones than bigger ones, that was for sure. I felt a hand grip my heart and then my anger rose. In our line of work, anger can get you killed, justified or not, but sometimes you can't help the way you react.

"Reaper?"

"Yeah, I see it."

Off to the left on its own was a single white cross. Even without asking, I knew what it was. I turned to Soran. "I'm sorry, my friend. This is a terrible loss for your people."

He nodded, tears in his eyes, and I felt myself feeling his pain.

We stared at the headstones for a while longer in somber silence then turned away and walked back to the horses. Then we left.

"Just to be clear, Mr. Kane, how many headstones do you figure were in the cemetery?" Holland asked.

"Over a hundred."

"And the white cross?"

"You figure it out."

CHAPTER 5

Like Soran said, it took us a day and a half to reach the airfield. The first night, we found a secure place to camp and then moved on just before daylight the following morning. We spent the next half day riding through oppressive heat until we reached our destination.

We set up camp behind a low ridge with a grove of trees backed up against it, which made it good for both humans and animals. Especially with air traffic.

Watching the airfield, we saw trucks come and go and soldiers walking the perimeter. A couple of Mig 25s took off for air patrols, and a truckload of Syrian soldiers arrived.

"We need to get in there," Knocker said to me. "See what they're up to."

"Did you see the extra hardpoints on the Migs?" I asked him.

He nodded. "Sure did. Just the place to attach canisters."

"Where do you figure they're storing the stuff?"

Knocker scanned the airfield through binoculars and paused looking at the large hangars not far from the control tower. "I have guards at the hangar on the right."

He passed me the glasses. I focused them on the hangar in question. There were two guards standing post outside. It was the only building on the airfield where guards were present. "That could be it."

"Do you think so?" Amira asked.

"There is only one way to find out."

She nodded.

"I saw you talking to Soran before we left," I said to her.

"Yes."

"Do you know him well?"

"He is my grandfather," Amira replied.

I wasn't expecting that. "What about your mother and father?"

"My mother was raped and killed by ISIS murderers. My father was taken away by Syrian soldiers and never seen again. Our lives are one constant fight."

"How did you get mixed up with trafficking people across the border?"

"Right place, right time, as you say."

I left it at that. The rest of the day, we watched, as I stated earlier. Then when the sun went down, the darkness brought with it the cold. It was beginning to be like an old friend. One that as much as you wanted, you just couldn't get rid of it. But comforting.

We started to prepare to infiltrate the airfield. We cleaned the dirt and grit out of our weapons. Divided up the explosives and detonators and used a mixture of dirt and water to make mud to daub on our faces. The plus side of infiltrating the airfield was that there were no fences.

We left Amira with the horses and slipped out into the darkness. I missed having NVGs, but the slim glimmer of moonlight helped a little in some ways but hindered in others. Keeping low, we crossed the open ground. Taking our time, we reached the halfway point when we scared a goat.

A single goat.

Which ran off.

And then blew up.

Fuck, we were in a minefield. We both froze and hugged the earth and hoped like hell there wasn't a mine beneath us.

Suddenly search lights swept the terrain where we lay unmoving, praying that the beams wouldn't pick us up.

My heart beat fiercely in my chest. I heard the approach of a vehicle, its headlights sweeping the minefield. The one positive about where we were, no one was in a hurry to come and look around.

I heard voices calling out. But couldn't understand what they were saying. Both Knocker and I lay there in silence, our breathing seemingly loud in the darkness. It seemed like an age before the Syrians climbed back into their vehicle and drove away. Then the searchlights stopped their seemingly endless sweeps.

I looked over at Knocker and said, "We need to go back and reassess."

"In case you didn't realize, we're in the middle of a fucking minefield," came his reply.

"Then get your knife out and start probing."

For the better part of a painful three hours, we used our knives to probe slowly through the top layer of dirt, searching for the deadly mines that lay beneath. At one point during the night, a helicopter lifted off from the airfield and swept low above us as it disappeared into the darkness. For a moment, I thought it was going to sweep the area looking for us. Then I admonished myself because there was no way they could have known we were there.

After those three hours, we slipped back into our layout position and found Amira where we'd left her.

"What happened?" she asked.

"A bloody goat," Knocker growled in a low voice. "We

scared the shit out of it, and it ran across and jumped on a fucking mine."

"What do you want to do now?" Amira asked.

"We lay up here tomorrow and then try again tomorrow night," I said.

Knocker looked at me as if I was stupid. "You want to go back through that damn minefield?"

"We'll have to find a way around it."

"Good fucking luck."

"If we want to finish what we started, we'll need to."

"Fine, but I'm getting some sleep. I've had too much excitement for one night."

"So, after all that, you still went back the next night?" German asked.

"That's right," I replied.

We spent the next day watching it again. Watching, and watching, and watching, and watching. Until we saw it. A way through to the airfield. We'd missed it at first, our gazes washing over it time and again. Then I saw it. A drain that was dry. And at the end of that drain was a concrete culvert. Without doubt, it was placed there to drain water from the airfield when it rained. We now had a way in.

"Bollocks," Knocker growled. "As sure as shit there'll be a bloody snake in that thing. Mark my words, Reaper."

I remembered the time he was referring to. He'd been crawling through a culvert and came face to face with a snake. The serpent had bitten him. We dragged him free of the concrete pipe and he'd been sure he was about to die. But luckily for him, it had been a dry bite and Knocker had survived.

"You will be fine," I assured him.

"Easy for you to say. You weren't the one that was bit by a damn snake last time."

I wasn't. I had to give him that. And if I had been, I probably would have had the same reaction. So, I gave him a few words of encouragement. "Suck it up, Princess."

Once again, after the sun had gone down, we prepared to leave. Two hours after dusk, we left our hide and started across the open ground toward the culvert. When we reached it, we crouched down and I grabbed a small flashlight that I'd carried with me.

It was too hard to carry our AK-12s through the culvert, so we had to leave them behind. Choosing only to take the handguns.

We shone the flashlight into the opening. There was sand along the bottom and what looked to be some type of roots hanging down. I looked back at my friend and said, "Follow me."

Lying on my stomach, I started to crawl through the narrow, cold pipe. It was slow progress. And at one point, the pipe narrowed and I thought that I might get stuck. It was a phobia that many people suffered from. Tight spaces. Getting stuck in there would have been anyone's worst nightmare.

We worked our way through the culvert for what seemed like hours, but in fact was only about thirty minutes. Finally, I breathed a sigh of relief as we reached the other end. I slid out into the drain and waited for Knocker to join me.

Once he was clear of the opening, I came up onto my knees and looked around. It had brought us out right at the edge of one of the runways. All we had to do now was get from there across the open ground to the hangar.

I looked back at Knocker and said softly, "Are you ready?"

"Let's go."

Keeping low, we ran across the hard concrete runway. On the other side, we crouched down into the long blades of grass, waiting. I scanned all around us and could see no patrols. So, once more, we came up and started running.

We reached the refueling truck and stopped. I tapped Knocker on the shoulder and said to him, "Place a charge here."

It took a couple of minutes, but once he was done, it was ready to go. From there, we sprinted across a road that ran alongside the runway and then around the back of the hangar.

There was a rear door there, so we tried it. It creaked open, and we slipped cautiously inside. It was barely lit by the false light of the moon from outside. It wasn't much and I was forced to use the flashlight.

Inside, there was an array of drums and crates. All had Russian writing stamped on them. I checked one of them out and found that it had poison stamped on it. "This could be what we're looking for."

We placed more explosives in and among the crates. And then we moved further through the hanger and found large canisters. These looked to be already armed with whatever the Russians were using.

"Did the canisters give you any indication of what they were?" Christine asked.

"No."

"Did you try to find out?"

"No."

"So, the complaint the Russians made could well be founded. You killed a number of their men for no reason and risked starting a war."

I stared at her. "Are you making judgments already, or would you like to hear more facts?" I asked impatiently.

"Continue."

We placed more charges in among the canisters and

armed them. We were about to leave when I turned and knocked over a small 20-liter drum. We both froze and waited for what happened next.

The two guards outside heard it crash to the ground and entered through the small door inside the large hangar doors.

Knocker and I hid, grabbing our suppressed handguns. The two guards used flashlights and their beams danced around in the darkness, illuminating everything they touched.

We shrunk down as one of the beams skipped across the area above us. They moved further into the hangar as they searched for whatever made the noise. Then, just as they were about to stumble onto us, Knocker and I both came up holding our handguns and fired twice each.

The suppressed sounds made low cracks. People call them silencers, but there's nothing silent about them. We hurried over and dragged their bodies into the dark shadows, then we shut off their flashlights and lay them next to them.

"How long before the charges go?" I asked.

"We've got just enough time to get into the culvert," Knocker replied.

"Then let's get the fuck out of here."

Leaving the same way we'd entered, through the rear door, we paused at the corner of the hanger to make sure the area was clear. Then we ran across to the fuel truck with the first of the charges had been planted. From there, we ran across the runway and then jumped down into a ditch at the mouth of the culvert.

Entering just as the first of the explosives blew, we felt the blast rock the ground around us. The culvert seemed to rain dust down upon us. We dragged ourselves through the narrow gap as a siren overhead blared its whining alarm. By the time we reached the other end, searchlights were roaming across the field. The hangar was burning brightly, orange flames leaping hundreds of feet into the air. Then I noticed something. Those who approached the fire began to stumble and fall as they were overcome by whatever was inside.

Normally, stuff like gas would have gone up with the flames neutralizing it. But this wasn't the case. I looked at Knocker and said, "We need to get the hell out of here now."

No one was worried about us. They were all looking at the fire, trying to help their comrades as they came to the invisible threat. Knocker and I ran as fast as we could toward the low ridge where Amira waited for us.

When we slid over the top and turned back to watch the fire, Amira appeared beside us. "What happened?"

"They had some new type of gas there. Stuff that the fire wasn't destroying."

Another explosion rocked the night as something else detonated inside the hangar. A large fireball rose like a giant orange mushroom cloud into the dark sky. I slapped Knocker on the shoulder and said, "Let's go. We need to be as far away from here as possible when the sun comes up."

"That's the best news I've heard all night."

"You say that the fire never affected the gas or whatever it was at all?" German asked.

I shook my head. "Not one bit."

"Astonishing."

"Is that what Sarah Nash was looking for?"

German looked hard at me. "Sarah who? I think we'll take a break here."

"Tell us what happened to the village?" German said.

"I was just coming to that before the break."

"We're listening now."

While we were gone, the Syrian army showed up. They just appeared the morning after we left. According to witnesses, at the time there were eight truckloads led by a general named Hosam Midani.

They pulled into the village and were greeted by Soran. For the most part, up until the Russians gassed the village, they had lived in relative peace with the Syrian government, choosing to fight ISIS instead. But that had changed, and Midani was there for a reason.

"Some foreigners came here. Where are they?"

Soran frowned, puzzled at how the general had come by such information. Thinking of his granddaughter, he lied. "I do not know what you mean."

"Are you sure?" Midani asked. "Consider your answer very carefully. The government does not look favorably on people who aid enemies of our glorious country."

"Whoever gave you such information lied to you, General."

But Midani wasn't convinced. He waved his arm and his men fanned out. Some guarding the villagers as they watched on, the others standing by Soran. "I will give you one more chance. Where are the interlopers?"

"They are not here. They never were."

Midani sighed, then drew his sidearm and shot Soran in the head. Soran dropped to the hard-packed earth and never moved. The Syrian general ran his gaze over the shocked onlookers. Among them was Ferhad. Midani said, "Hang his body and let it be a reminder of what happens to those who conspire against the government. Hang two more beside him."

And that's what he did. His men killed two more villagers randomly and hung their bodies up beside Soran before leaving.

"That was it?" German asked.

"That was enough."

"Enough to make you change your mission again, obviously," Christine Ryan stated.

"That was one of the factors."

When we arrived back at the village, the bodies were still there. Amira leaped from her horse and ran to them, falling to her knees as she wept uncontrollably for her grandfather. I looked for Ferhad. "What happened?"

"General Hosam Midani," he informed me.

"Who is he?"

"He is the commander for this region. He came here because you had come here."

I was confused. "How did he know we were here?"

"How do you think?" he spat. "Someone told him."

I looked around at the gathering crowd. Somewhere among them was a traitor. Then something else occurred to me. What if the same person who betrayed us also betrayed Sarah Nash? I turned to Knocker. "I have a job for you?"

"Oh, aye?"

"Someone among these people is a traitor. Find them."

He gave me a cold grin and said, "With fucking pleasure."

"I need them alive, Knocker. I can't get answers if they're not."

"How alive?"

"Shit, just find them."

I turned my attention back to Amira. I helped cut the bodies down and then bury them. It was the least I could do for what they had done for us. Once we were finished, I left Amira to her grief.

"He was a tough old man," Ferhad told me later. "He led his people in the fight against ISIS. He led fifty fighters and allied with United States soldiers who fought with us. Come, I'll show you something."

He took me to a large building in the center of the village. Once we were inside, he walked over to the far wall and lifted a mat on the floor. Beneath it was a small wooden door. He opened—"

"What has this got to do with anything?" Holland interrupted.

"I think it's important that you know what kind of man he was," I stated. "May I continue?"

"Fine."

Ferhad opened the trapdoor and revealed a small wooden box inside. He took it out, and inside, there were three military patches. I stared at them. Two were US issue, the other was British. "Each one was given to him as a mark of respect for his bravery in battle. They did not give us medals. Especially since we are classed as terrorists. So, he was given these. The British one came after he rode into immense gunfire and pulled out a soldier from the SAS."

"He was a very brave man."

"Yes, he was."

After two hours of asking questions and observing, Knocker found what we were looking for then tracked me down near one of the houses in the shade. Here."

He tossed me a satellite phone. "Where did you get that?"

"From the digs of our friendly neighborhood squealer."

"Who?"

"You are going to love this, Reaper."

Moments later I was looking at the man who we suspected of being the informer. It was Ferhad.

CHAPTER 6

"HE WAS WITH YOU ALL THAT TIME AND YOU HAD NO IDEA HE WAS a traitor?" Christine Ryan asked. There was more than a hint of condescension in her voice.

Knocker grinned coldly. "You work for the British government, how's that working out?"

What he was referring to will become clearer later. But for now...

Holland sighed impatiently. "Yes, yes, continue or we'll be here all day."

I placed the muzzle of my handgun against the base of Ferhad's skull and said, "Come with us, asshole. We have some questions for you."

He froze. "What is happening?"

"You'll find out."

We took him to a vacant mudbrick abode and shoved him inside. He whirled around and Knocker hit him square in the face, drawing blood. "Back the fuck off."

"Why are you doing this?" Ferhad demanded.

I threw the satellite phone at him. I wasn't subtle about it and the flying brick hit him in the head. "Maybe you want to explain why you have an encrypted sat phone."

"It isn't mine. I've never seen it before."

Knocker stepped in close and hit him in the stomach, doubling him over. He grabbed a handful of greasy hair and lifted Ferhad's head. "Try again. It came from your stuff."

"I-I tell you, I have never seen it before," he gasped. "Someone must have put it there."

"Bollocks," Knocker growled.

"Why would I tell you there was a traitor among us if I was the one?" he asked.

He was right, but at that point, I didn't care. "Maybe to throw suspicion off you," I replied.

Knocker hit him again and even more blood flowed. "I can do this all day, mate. The phone says you're the prick who's doing it. Did you do the same to the reporter?"

"No."

"Huh? I bet you did. She was getting too close to the truth. Who did you tell? The Syrians? The Russians?"

"No!"

"Who?"

"No one. It isn't mine."

I tugged on Knocker's sleeve and pulled him away. "He could be telling the truth."

"OK, say that he is. Who else could it be?"

I turned to Ferhad. "Who else could it be?"

"I do not know. But it isn't me."

"What is happening here?" Amira had found us. She saw Ferhad. "What are you doing?"

She stepped past me to protect Ferhad. "Let him go."

"He was found in possession of a sat phone," I told her. "It looks like your man is a traitor."

"Impossible. We have known each other since we were children. Ferhad would do no such thing."

"Really? Then where did it come from?" I asked her.

"Someone must have put it there. I would trust Ferhad with my life and have done so on many occasions."

"Then who, damn it? Whoever it was got your grandfather killed and Sarah Nash as well."

"There, you see!" Amira exclaimed.

"See what?"

"The reporter died while we were in Turkey." She paused. Then, "Are you saying that she was the target of the gassing attack?"

"It seems to be a coincidence that when we show up, the Syrians come, and when Sarah Nash is here looking into whatever it was, the village suffers a gas attack."

"Well, whoever it was obviously survived the attack," Amira said.

"Obviously."

She stared at me. "Give me the phone and two hours and I will find out who the real traitor is. If I cannot, I will shoot Ferhad myself."

I nodded. "Fine. Until then, Knocker will keep a close eye on him."

We were wrong about Ferhad. It wasn't him at all, and when Amira came to us a couple of hours later, she had the name of the one responsible.

"It is Yaran."

"Who is he?"

"One of the village elders. The one who doesn't like you."

"How do you know it's him?" Knocker asked.

She held up the sat phone. "I called a friend. She said to say hello, by the way."

"Shit," Knocker growled with a shake of his head.

"Our friend was able to trace all calls made on the phone for the last year. Most of them terminated with General Hosam Midani. She was then able to dig deeper, and Yaran suddenly came to the top of the shit pile."

"We should go and talk to him."

He was smoking, seated in the shade of a building when we found him. He saw us coming and remained unmoved at our approach. He puffed on his cigarette and blew out a large cloud of smoke. When we were almost upon him, Yaran surprised us. He obviously knew we were onto him. His plan to frame Ferhad hadn't worked. From the folds of his clothing, he took a handgun, placed it under his chin, and blew his own brains out.

"That fucked that," Knocker said.

I searched his pockets and found nothing. I don't really know what I expected. I looked at Amira. "Can you ask around to see if anything was left behind from the reporter?"

"Why?"

"Maybe there might be something we don't know about. Do you know where she slept?"

Amira turned to one of the villagers who had gathered around. She said something I couldn't understand and got an answer. "Come with me."

Following her to a small mud brick house, we went inside and found it empty. Amira said, "She stayed in here."

I looked at Knocker. "Start in one of the rooms."

We went through the house room by room—not that there were many—searching meticulously for anything. It was then that Knocker found a small piece of paper with hand-scrawled writing on it saying, *HE'S HERE*.

I looked at Knocker. "Who's here?"

"That was why she was there, wasn't it?" I said to them. "She was looking for him. For them."

The three of them just stared at us.

"We could have been told instead of going in blind."

Still, they said nothing, so I kept going.

It was then that we made another decision to go off-book. I turned to Knocker and said, "We go after Midani. Find out what's happening and take him out."

"Sounds good to me."

I asked Amira, "Where can we find the general?"

"He has a base in a town forty miles from here."

"Then what are we waiting for?"

Later that day we left, this time by truck, to cover the distance a lot quicker. That and to make sure it would be dark when we got there.

The road was rough, dirt with deep ruts, which tried their best to shake the shit out of the truck, so it fell apart.

Amira drove because she knew where she was going. The road was clear of traffic all the way.

An hour after dark, the lights from the village appeared. Amira eased the truck to a stop off the road. "His headquarters are in the center of the town. The barracks are on the far side of town. You should get out here and go in on foot. I will drive in and park on the outskirts of town on this side. When you are done, meet me there. If it all goes bad, I will come for you."

Getting out of the truck, we started toward the lights. At the edge of town, we stuck to the narrow alleys, which proved to be like rabbit warrens. Dogs barked in the night and once a voice shouted, presumably telling them to be quiet.

As we crept closer to the center of town, the patrols became more frequent. We were about to cross an intersection when Knocker grabbed my arm, stopping me. "To the left," he whispered.

I looked but saw nothing. After a couple of moments of intense staring, I saw the faint glow of a cigarette tip in the shadows. Someone was waiting there.

So, we waited where we were. A few minutes later, a man came along the street and the other one stepped out into the moonlight. They greeted each other and walked along the street.

Once they were gone, we crossed and disappeared into another alley.

It took thirty minutes of slow going, but eventually, we

reached the place where we were meant to be. We hid in the shadows and watched for a further twenty minutes. There were two guards outside the main entrance. There had to be more inside the double-floored building but there was no way of knowing until we got in there.

"You ready?" I asked Knocker.

"Let's do it, Reaper."

Our AK-12s came up and we sighted on the guards. It was a maneuver we'd completed many times. I gave the go-ahead and we shot them both.

Crossing the street at a run, we dragged them around the side of the building. Then we breached.

The inside was lit with dull orange light, the spinoff of a poor power source. The floor was covered in blue and white vinyl. To the right of the entry hall was a desk. At that desk was a soldier, hunched over, tired of doing paperwork.

Instantly awake, his head snapped up, and because he was on Knocker's side as we cleared, it fell to him to take the shot.

The soldier died slumped in his seat, chest bloody from the two bullet holes. I moved left toward a door while Knocker swept the stairwell to make sure it was clear. For a moment, he backtracked and locked the door.

I lowered the AK-12 and took out the suppressed handgun I carried before I opened my door. Entering the room, I found two soldiers seated at a table. I shot both with a shot each to the head.

I made sure there was no one else and went back out to the entry hall. I said to Knocker, "Up or down?"

"Up, generals like being on top of things."

Taking the stairs two at a time, we went up. We took the careless route, looking at the doors instead of clearing the rooms as we sought the one we wanted.

It was at the end of the hallway, facing along it. The one with a small gold plaque on it. I opened it and Knocker went through. I heard his weapon's muffled crack and a body hit the floor.

I followed him in and saw the general sitting behind his desk, a look of surprise on his face. On the floor was another soldier. Maybe his adjutant.

"Are you Midani?" I asked him.

He just stared at me.

Knocker tried and the man nodded.

"Ask him why the reporter was killed."

Knocker repeated the question and the general rattled off a reply. "He says he doesn't know about a reporter."

"What about the gassing of the village?"

Knocker repeated my question again. Midani replied.

"He says that had nothing to do with him. That was the Russians."

"We fucking know that. Why?"

The question was asked. "He doesn't know."

"What about the old man? Why were they looking for us?" I asked.

"He says he was just following orders."

"Was killing the old man orders?" I hissed in a low voice.

Midani said nothing.

"Come on, Reaper, let's get the fuck out of here, he knows nothing."

"He must know something."

The general said something. I looked at Knocker. "What did he say?"

"We just follow his orders."

"Whose orders? The president?"

Midani went silent again. Knocker peered out into the hallway. It was all clear, but if we lingered, we would eventually be discovered. As much as I wanted answers, I wanted to get caught less, so I shot him twice in the chest and once in the head.

Then we got the hell out of there.

"It seems to me, Mr. Kane, that you have a tendency to commit murder," Holland said to me.

"I do what I have to do to survive, Mr. Holland. Nothing more. This is the world of black ops, not civvy street."

"All of that for nothing," Christine Ryan pointed out.

"It wasn't for nothing," Knocker replied. "We learned there was someone behind the scenes pulling the strings. That same person had Sarah Nash murdered and tried to have us killed as well."

German flicked through the papers on the table. "Where did you go next?"

We met up with Amira on the edge of town like she told us to. She was there waiting. We'd had to avoid some patrols around the town, but their security was reasonably slack. By the time we'd climbed into the truck, the alarm was being raised.

But by then, it was too late.

We drove north in the truck, not wanting to go back to the village. We headed for a refugee camp close to the Turkish border. From there, we would get across and go home. Well, that was the plan.

We chose to travel by night and lay up during the day. The following day, we were hiding in a wadi, the truck out of sight. Amira sat beside me and said, "Did you make the pig suffer?"

I shook my head. "No. There wasn't time."

"Pity. What did he tell you?"

"Not much, but he alluded to someone behind the scenes pulling the strings."

"But not who?"

"No."

Knocker slid down the wadi bank with a look of concern on his face. "You should look at this."

I climbed the bank, as did the others. We then watched a column of trucks come along the road. Some were military trucks, others were civilian transport trucks. I took up the binoculars I had and peered through them. After a few minutes, I said, "They're Syrian transports, but they're not Syrians."

"Russian?" Knocker wondered.

"Possibly. But where are they headed? Amira, what do you think?"

"The only thing in that direction is our village."

We all remained silent as we watched the column continue past. Once they were gone, the rumbling from the motors fell silent. "Reaper, are you thinking what I'm thinking?"

"That we need to find out what they're up to. They can only be headed for the village."

"And with all that equipment and firepower, I'm thinking they mean to stay."

I sighed. "Why isn't anything just simple?"

We moved again just after dark. This time, we headed for the village. Found a place to lay up and observe what was happening. Observe the bloodbath.

The gunfire reached out across the darkness, along with the screams and cries of pain. Using the binoculars and by the light of multiple fires, I could see the soldiers murdering the villagers. I saw one man on his knees pleading to a soldier and then shot in the head. I saw another soldier setting fire to buildings with a flamethrower then he turned it on a woman and her child.

All the while, my anger rose because I could do nothing to help them.

The soldiers were being directed by a man wearing desert fatigues. He wasn't taking part in the slaughter, just giving directions. As I watched, I tried to comprehend why they would do this to the village twice. It was plain genocide.

Then I saw him standing casually off to one side. He wasn't dressed like the soldiers. He wore civilian clothes and a flat-brimmed hat. This was the man in charge.

More gunfire rattled throughout the night, and it made me feel sick to see the carnage below. Knocker had seen enough, and Amira sat at the base of the slope, hands over her ears, and wept.

Throughout it all, I saw a young man dragged across an open expanse of ground in the village and dropped. He looked up at his executioner and I caught a glimpse of his face. It was Ferhad. The soldier shot him twice.

I muttered a curse and was about to slide back down the slope when I caught sight of the man again. And this time, he was looking right at me.

Sliding back down the slope, I stopped beside Knocker and Amira. "We need to go."

"Now?" Knocker asked.

"Yes, now. They know we're here."

"What? It's bloody dark, mate. How the fuck could they know we're here?"

"I don't know, but he does."

"He?"

"Yes, he. I'll tell you later. Now, let's move."

"What about my people?"

"I'm sorry, Amira, but it's too late for that. Besides, we could do nothing anyway. The Russians would have us at a big disadvantage. All we can do right now is survive."

Minutes later, we were back in the truck and running for the refugee camp.

"Who was the man you saw?" German asked.

"I don't know—I mean, I do now, but at the time I had no idea."

"Then how did you know he was Russian?"

"Calculated guess. That and the fact he was with Russian Special Forces."

"Then how did you know they were Russian if you didn't know he was?" Holland asked.

"Experience."

The commander of the special forces had been called Chuzhkov. He'd led them into the village the first time when they gassed it. Originally, they'd thought the villagers were all dead, or at least moved on. However, when word came that we were there, he and his men had been mobilized again to finish the job. And to kill us.

We weren't there, but that didn't stop them. When he approached the commander, he saw him looking into the darkness. "Are you all right, Comrade?"

"They are out there," he said, his gaze unwavering.

"Who?"

"The ones we needed to kill."

"How can you be sure?"

"I know."

"I will send out a patrol."

"No, wait until morning. Clean out the village first and burn the bodies. Work needs to start as soon as possible."

Chuzhkov nodded. "Yes, Comrade."

By the time the patrol had been dispatched, we were long gone.

In fact, we were only about twenty miles from the refugee camp. Driving a truck was a lot different to riding horses.

When the camp appeared, it was like a sea of tents

dotted across the countryside. Most of the refugees in the camp had been driven north when ISIS was prevalent in Syria and the rebels were fighting the Syrian government.

After everything had quietened down, most of them had nowhere to go. No homes, for they were all destroyed when cities and towns were turned into strongholds and then taken back by force. Daily bombing raids saw to that.

At its peak, there were almost a hundred thousand in this camp. There were others that were much bigger. This one now housed perhaps fifty thousand. Mostly Kurdish people or families who were displaced.

We drove into the camp and were met by a man—a Brit, as luck would have it—wearing an armband which identified him as a UN official. "What can I do for you?" he asked.

"We're just passing through," I told him. "Thought we might see if we could stay the night."

He stared at us, at our kit and weapons. "I don't know if that would be wise."

"Listen, we just witnessed a village being slaughtered by Russian Special Forces. All we want to do is have a rest and get back to report it. We work for the British government."

He still didn't like the idea. "The far side of the camp has vacant tents. Rest there, but you need to be gone come morning."

I nodded. "Thank you."

CHAPTER 7

We found a couple spare tents over where he told us to go. He hadn't given his name, and we didn't ask. Things are often better that way. Knocker and I bunked in together, and Amira was in the tent beside us. There were cots inside, but that was it. No blankets, no other comforts of any kind. I figured they'd been taken for other refugees.

Sitting on my cot, I reached into my pack and found a couple of muesli bars. I tossed one to Knocker, who caught it and tore it open. He took a bite and said, "I could never see nutritional value in one of these things except for birds. And I'm not a bird."

He was right, for crap they were tasteless.

He said, "What are we going to do, Reaper? This mission has been pretty much a clusterfuck from the start. We're being used again."

I nodded. Once more, my friend's deep insights into our situation were right.

"Thanks, Reaper."

"You're welcome."

I said, "Once we're back in Turkey, we'll reach out to

Holly Smith and get her to get us out of here. We'll fill her in and try to get some answers about Sarah Nash."

"What about him?"

"It would be good to know who he is. Maybe Holly will know."

Night fell, and we lay back on our cots fully clothed and went to sleep. Knocker snored for a while, and I was sure I joined him, only to be woken by thunder.

I was in a sleep-muddled haze when I first heard it. Somewhere in the distance, the deep rumble of an approaching storm. It seemed to be moving fast. The next rumble I heard was closer. Much closer. In actual fact, it sounded like a—

"Sonic Boom! Get up, Knocker, we've got incoming."

He came to his feet and grabbed his AK-12 and body armor. I was already shrugging into mine. The next boom was almost overhead as the Mig-25 howled over us, leaving a trail of orange mushrooms from the ordnance it had dropped.

We emerged from the tent and from our position on the hill, could see the line of explosions running through the camp.

"Motherfucker," Knocker snarled.

"Get Amira—get down!"

The line of explosions kept coming toward us without ceasing. We threw ourselves to the ground as the last one exploded close enough to feel its heat.

I scrambled to my feet and stared at the carnage around us. Amira emerged from her tent. "What is happening?"

"The camp is being—"

My voice was drowned out by a second Mig. This one made its run perpendicular to the previous one. Once again, it was chased by more explosions.

"Fucking cluster bombs," Knocker growled. "We need to get out of here."

"Why are they doing this?" Amira asked.

I said, "Three guesses, but you'll only need one."

"Us? They're doing this because of us?"

"No kill like a lucky one. Move."

Amira climbed into the truck, and I was about to follow when we heard the gunfire. It was coming from the far side of the camp. Knocker heard it too. He looked at me. "Reaper—"

However, I had already turned and started running.

"Shit a brick," Knocker growled and started following me.

We were running to the sound of the guns. Sounds noble, doesn't it? But when you're outnumbered, it's just plain stupid. However, people were dying. Innocent people who couldn't protect themselves, and I'd already seen enough of it. So, I kept running.

All around me tents were burning, charred and dismembered bodies lay beside them. The sound of gunfire grew closer, and I slowed down. Knocker attached himself to my six, covering me as I pressed forward.

The first shooter appeared on my right, dressed in military fatigues, wearing a ski mask pulled down over his face. "Contact front."

My AK came up slightly and I fired, hitting him in the throat and face as I tried to avoid the body armor he wore. Another sign he was Russian Spec Ops. He grunted and fell. Almost immediately, he was replaced by another. I fired again. This time, the rounds were caught by his chest plate. He sat down hard, and I pressed forward and put a bullet in his head.

"Contact right!" Knocker cried out, and I threw myself sideways as he opened fire. "Clear."

As it turned out, the camp had suddenly become a target-rich environment. I shot two more men, one was forcing himself on a woman. I walked up behind him and shot him in the back of the head with my handgun.

We continued our search for more targets and Knocker said, "What the hell are we doing, Reaper?"

"Killing bad guys," I replied and shot another man. I dropped out an empty magazine and reloaded. "That and trying to save lives. Just—"

A killer hit me from the side and we both went down in a tangle of arms and legs. His momentum carried him over me, and I rolled with him, coming up on top. I hit him in the face three times with my elbow. The blows knocked him stupid, giving me enough time to pull my handgun and shoot him in the head.

Knocker dragged me to my feet. "You need to get your shit together. Stupid moves like that will get you killed."

"Really? How about you take point?"

He stepped forward. "Thought you would never ask."

I followed him, watching our six. We passed between more burning tents, and at one point, he was almost knocked over by fleeing refugees.

A loud roar overhead signaled the passing of another Mig-25. The boom seemed to vibrate through my body. Ahead of me, Knocker snapped his weapon around but held his fire. A figure was stumbling toward him, and it took a moment to realize that it was the UN guy.

He had blood running down his face and part of his shirt was burned off his right shoulder. He waved at us. "Go! Go back, they're coming this—"

The rattle of automatic gun fire ripped through the air, and he stumbled and fell onto his face.

His fall cleared our line of sight so we could see the shooters coming toward us.

Three of them.

Both Knocker and I opened fire at the same time. The

three Russians stopped in their tracks as though they'd walked into an invisible fist. They fell to the ground, and Knocker pressed forward, making sure that they were out of the fight.

I heard the approach of another Mig-25, and it was gone before the trailing sound. This time, the screaming jet had dropped more bombs, and the CRUMP-CRUMP-CRUMP of their detonations steadily moved toward us.

We both hit the ground and covered our heads. Not that it would do a lot of good if one of the cluster bombs dropped too close anyway. Maybe it was a feel-safe thing.

The earth moved for us both once more, and not in a good way. Shrapnel and flames exploded through the air, and more people died. A human torch emerged into the open and I saw that it was a Russian. These people were beyond caring who they killed.

I grabbed Knocker and said, "We need to clear the camp. Follow me. It's time to go."

As we retreated the way we'd come, we came across a child. There was a woman draped over her, protecting her. It was a woman we both knew.

Amira. And she was dead.

"What happened to her?" Christine Ryan asked.

"She'd been shot."

"Trying to protect the child?"

"Maybe. She had been shot twice in the chest. The kid was killed after her. Maybe so there were no witnesses."

"Who would do that?"

"The same person who didn't want anyone to know he was there."

When daylight came, the fires had died down, and the Russians, along with their planes, were gone. Refugees were wandering around as though in a trance, and a force of SAS operators had arrived from out of the Syrian landscape to secure the camp and assist in any way they could.

They were led by a sergeant who went by the name of Wilkes. In all, there were ten of them in the patrol, including two medics who went to work right away.

Meanwhile, I had a chat with Wilkes. "What happened?"

"Russian Special Forces and fighter bombers," I told him.

"We were getting reports of Ivans in the area, but to do this is bloody crazy."

"Yeah, well, they're a few less than what they were."

"Good for you guys."

"You wouldn't have a secure sat phone we could use?" I asked him.

"For?"

"Call head shed."

"Yeah, I think we can come up with something."

Ten minutes later, I was talking to Holly Smith.

"You fucking screwed us," I said to her.

"What do you mean?" she asked.

I gave her a run down on everything. When I was finished, she asked, "Are you sure Nash was MI6?"

"Who else could she be?" I replied, annoyed that she'd dismissed everything else to focus on that one thing. "She was here looking for someone. Whether it was official or otherwise, I don't know."

"Give me a moment. I'll call you back."

I waited twenty minutes before she called. "She was there observing Russian activity. That's all. We heard they were up to something, but we didn't know what. Then they gassed the village and contact was lost. Whatever she found, we have no idea."

"Wait, you knew she was here?"

"Not right off. Only after you had left."

"Why didn't you say something?"

"I was told not to. If she was there, you would find her."

"What do you want us to do now?"

"Come in, mission is over."

"Wait," German said. "You were ordered to come in by your handler?"

"Yes."

"And you disobeyed that order?"

"Not right off."

I asked her about the Russian guy we saw. Holly told me he was possibly the special forces commander overseeing things. But I wasn't convinced. "Just come in, I'll get you out of Syria. Go with the SAS guys."

It was about that time I decided that to get the answers we wanted, I knew what we would have to do. I disconnected the call and said to Knocker, "We're going back."

"Yeah, I knew we would be."

Then I asked Wilkes for a sat phone to take with us. He told me he didn't have one to spare, so we topped up our ammo and went back.

"That's when we disobeyed orders."

We were taking the truck, topping it off with fuel and then headed back south. The SAS blokes gave us intel about the Russians having a camp around one hundred kilometers southeast. That was the way we headed.

The first night, we found a wadi just before dawn and camped there for the day. The road was quiet, and after dark, we packed up and started off again.

We traversed the terrain, trying to stay off the roads. Then, just after midnight, we hit a hole and broke an axle on the truck.

Knocker kicked the wheel and said, "Looks like we walk the rest of the way, Reaper."

I took out a map and used my flashlight to go over it. "By

my calculations, we're about ten klicks short of where we want to be."

"Doesn't seem so bad when you say it quickly like that."

"Well, we're not getting any closer standing here jawing about it," I replied. "If we push hard enough, we'll make it by dawn."

So, we began walking through the night, leaving the broken truck where it was. There was some moonlight to walk by, which made the going a little easier. At one point, we had to take shelter when we disturbed a herd of goats. As luck would have it, the shepherd was with them.

Once they settled, we continued until a cluster of lights in the distance told us we had made it.

Knocker and I found a place to lay up and observe the camp for the day. We wanted to get the lay of the land before we went in the next night.

When the sun came up, it was hidden by a gray overcast for the first few hours. Activity slowly started to grow as the daylight hours progressed. We lay there taking turns watching and learning. I was asleep just after midday when Knocker woke me from a dream about being on a cruise ship with my sister.

"Reaper, you need to take a look at this."

I rolled over and moved into a position where I could use the binoculars to observe the camp. "What am I looking at?"

"Near the truck. They just arrived."

The binoculars swept to the left and I saw them. One man I didn't know. He was dressed in civilian clothes. The other I'd seen the night at the village. It was him. "Motherfucker."

"That's one way of describing him," Knocker said. "There are a few other choice words I would have used."

"We go tonight."

"Sounds good to me."

Waiting for the sun to go down, we added a few more hours after that. Knocker took point. I wasn't embarrassed to admit he was a much better operator than I was. And I thought of myself as good.

We reached the perimeter fence and cut our way through. From our surveillance, we had our target in a building near what looked to be a communications hut.

Using the shadows, we crept further in. Knocker slid under a truck, and I followed him. We remained there while a patrol passed by, then slid out. The main thing to remember was we had to remain undetected. Which we were doing well.

Or so we thought.

We were passing across an open part of the base, thinking there was no one around when floodlights came on and lit us up like a damn Christmas tree.

"STOP THERE OR WE WILL OPEN FIRE!" the megaphone someone was holding screeched at us.

Knocker and I froze. "Looks like we're fucked, Reaper."

I nodded. "Put our weapons down. While we're breathing, we're still in this."

"Unless the guy we're after is a real cunt."

Christine Ryan glared at me. I shrugged.

Knocker said, "Just for the record, he was a cunt."

She rolled her eyes.

I continued.

The man we'd gone in after emerged from behind the lit perimeter along with his special forces commander. He looked smug. "Comrade Chuzhkov, have your men disarm them."

Chuzhkov, the special forces commander, directed a few of his men forward and they took all our weapons. Once they were done, they forced us to our knees and had us lock our hands behind our heads. Uncomfortable as shit.

"Welcome, gentlemen," the commander said to us.

"The commander?" German asked.

I nodded. "Commander, Russian. You have to understand, at this point, we had no idea who he was."

German sighed. "Fine, if you must. Carry on."

The Russian stepped closer to us and asked us our names. At this point, I was able to get a better look at him. Lined face, almost pure gray hair, maybe late sixties. Product of the Cold War. Carried himself like an old-school officer.

"Your names?" he asked again.

I looked at him. "Billy."

"Joel," Knocker added.

For a strait-laced kind of guy, he took it in his stride. "Let me guess, you didn't start the fire?"

I shrugged. "Been known to start a few."

"Started one the other night," Knocker added. "Not as big as yours though. Murdering prick."

Chuzhkov stepped forward and kicked Knocker in the stomach. He fell forward, gasping for air. I glared at the special forces commander and spat at him. What the hell, why not? He was an asshole.

So, he kicked me too.

"It is getting late," the Russian said. "Lock them up and I will question them tomorrow."

We were dragged to our feet, led away, and locked up in a small building with bars on the windows and a solid wood door. Once we were locked away, I said to Knocker, "What have you got?"

"Nothing, the bastards bloody cleaned me out. You?"

"Yeah, me too."

I walked around the prison cell once and sat down out of

the light coming through the window, back against the wall. "Get some sleep. We'll see what washes out in the morning."

CHAPTER 8

After years of operating, a person learns to get sleep where and when they can. Sometimes it isn't easy. Other times, it's like rolling off a log. But when you have a partner that snores like a chainsaw cutting logs, it's almost impossible.

I listened to the noises outside. Vehicles coming and going. A helicopter came in and stayed. I could hear guards talking as they walked past, one complaining about how their commander didn't like him because he screwed a drill.

Yes, I can understand Russian, along with a few other languages that were tortured into me by my bosses in the spec ops world.

I caught minutes of sleep here and there. Most of them after I'd thrown pebbles at Knocker for snoring. But after a while he'd go back to it, so I gave up.

Eventually, the sun came up and activity increased around the camp. My stomach growled as it became aware of the time, and water wouldn't have gone astray either. My mouth felt as though it had a good portion of dust in it.

Knocker groaned and cracked open an eye. "Shit,

morning already. Man, I had a good sleep. Except for the bugs. Some of the bastards kept hitting me in the face."

"Really?"

"How about you, Reaper? You sleep all right?"

"Like a log, Raymond."

His other eye snapped open at me using his name. "What?"

I closed my eyes and said, "Never mind."

"What do you figure they're going to do with us?" Knocker opined.

I sighed. Even awake he was trying to ruin my damn sleep. "Shoot us and throw us in a wash," I snapped curtly.

"Who do you figure the Russian is?"

"I don't know."

"He looks old school," Knocker said. "Former officer, maybe."

"Maybe."

"I guess we'll find out."

"I guess we will," I replied without opening my eyes.

It took two more hours before they came and got us. Four men, all armed to the teeth. They didn't look so happy. Maybe it was because we'd handed their asses to them the few nights before.

They zippy-tied our hands behind our backs before marching us across a large parade ground and into a building with separate rooms. The Russian was in there waiting for us, along with the special forces commander. But there was also another man. This one wore a suit. He was Syrian.

This was a man I knew. He was the Syrian defense minister. His name was Hussain Anez. He glared at us, unhappy with our intrusion into his country. After a moment, he said, "These are the men responsible?"

"How did you know he was the Syrian defense minister?" German asked me.

"I'd seen him often enough over the years on television. Especially after he murdered a bunch of ISIS women. The war brides who were lured into the country."

"If they didn't go, they'd still be alive," Christine Ryan said without emotion.

"I'm not saying they would be, just answering the question you asked."

They went silent. I glanced at my watch and continued once more.

"That's them," the Russian replied. "They are very good at what they do. The question is, what is it they are doing?"

Anez stared at me and asked, "Why are you in my country?"

"We got lost," I replied.

Chuzhkov stepped forward and slapped me across the face. I stared at him and said nothing. He put his face close to mine, his teeth never even parted when he said, "Answer the man."

"Did I tell you I'm fucking hopeless at navigating?" Knocker said. "We took a wrong turn then, before I'd even realized, we were hopelessly lost."

"Tie them to the chairs," the Russian said.

Chuzhkov had two of his men drag the chairs over and we were forced to sit on them. We were then bound to them, and the Russian walked over to us and stood no more than a foot away. "You can make this easy or hard upon yourself," he said.

"Seems we've been in this predicament recently," I observed.

"Before we get started, do you have water?" Knocker asked. "I'm as dry as a fucking desert."

"Why are you here?" the Russian asked again, ignoring the request.

"Did you order the gas attack on the village?" I countered.

He stared at me. "Did you find what you were looking for?"

"Did Sarah Nash?" A flicker in his left eye. I pushed my luck. "Was she the target, or the village, or both? How about you, Hussain? Did you order it?"

His eyes widened, fear gripping his heart at my use of his name."

"Are you here for me? Is that it? Are you both assassins?"

"Shut up, you fool," the Russian snapped. "They are not here for you."

"Well, we know who is in command," I said.

Chuzhkov stepped forward and slapped me open-handed across the face. I tasted blood from the inside of my cheek cutting on a tooth. I spat blood on the floor and sat up, grinning. "That's one, motherfucker."

He hit me again.

Once more, I spat blood on the floor and straightened up. "Two, motherfucker."

The special forces commander placed his face close to mine. "Two what, motherfucker?"

I headbutted him across the bridge of his nose hard enough to break it and sit him on his ass. "Two is one chance more than I'd give anyone else, asshole."

Howling in rage, he came to his feet, drawing his sidearm. He was about to shoot me in his fit of anger when the Russian stopped him.

"Enough. Go and get yourself cleaned up, Boris."

I could see in Chuzhkov's eyes that he really wanted to kill me, but something held him back. Maybe it was the Russian. With a curse, he left the room. I looked at the Russian and said, "What would you have done if he'd shot me?"

The man produced his own weapon. "I would have killed him too."

"OK."

"Do I have to ask you again or will you answer the question?"

"We were sent to see if you—the Syrians and Russians—were using chemical weapons," I said.

"I see."

"We had no idea about the journalist until we reached the village."

The Russian nodded. "I'm thinking that you also know that the woman was not a journalist."

"Any idea how he knew?" I asked the interrogation panel. "He knew she was MI6. Was her presence kept internally? If it was, it pointed to a fox in the henhouse."

"That's a fucking mole for the uneducated," Knocker pointed out to them.

"But I guess you know that now. But not then, huh? Embarrassing somewhat."

"Just keep going," Christine Ryan snapped.

"We do now," I replied.

"The airfield? The explosions, that was you as well."

"You know it was," I said.

"Why?"

"Why what?"

"Why didn't you just leave?"

"I was pissed off."

The Russian shook his head. "No, I do not think so. Maybe it was like the woman. You were sent here looking for me."

"Someone likes looking at himself in the mirror," Knocker growled.

I shook my head. "We never knew about you until later. Shit, we don't even know who you are? You got a name?"

He just smiled coldly and kept on. "General Midani?"

I nodded again. "He said he was following orders. Were they yours?"

The Russian just stared at me.

I thought for a moment. "The village was two-fold, wasn't it? First the gas attack to kill the civilians, but the MI6 officer was a bonus. Did she see something she wasn't meant to? Find something out? Was it you she saw? She left a note saying, he's here."

The Russian remained silent again. He was trying to find out what I knew, and I was willingly giving it to him. If I didn't, they would torture it out of us, and we'd be in no shape to escape when the time came.

"Then we came along, and you sent Midani after us, but we weren't there, and he killed Soran. Then we saw you again at the village. You and your men murdering them all. But somehow, you knew we were not there. You found out where we went and attacked the refugee camp. You knew after that we would come after you and you set the trap. How am I doing?"

The Russian nodded. "You seem competent enough. It is a shame I'm going to have to kill you."

But I hadn't played my hole card yet. "Tell me, why don't you want anyone to know you are here? Why is one of the old guard in Syria? Former KGB, right? Maybe even a general from the USSR days? What would entice you out of your hole?"

"You wonder too much," the Russian replied, the spirit of the game gone.

"You don't want to play anymore?"

"No, we will take you out into the desert and shoot you tomorrow."

"Just like that?"

"Yes."

"Kill them now," Anez said.

"I will have them killed when I am ready. Besides, I might want to ask them more questions."

"Is it oil?" I asked, throwing a Hail Mary out there.

The Russian stared at me. The Syrian gave it away.

"Oil?" asked German. "There is oil under the village and that was why they killed them all? Why they killed Nash?"

"I don't know why Nash was there, but what they were up to, I'm sure she stumbled onto it. Onto him anyway, and he didn't want anyone to know he was there. As for the oil, it was the first part of the plan," I said. "As you will see. They needed the oil."

They took us back to our cell and locked us in. Knocker looked at me and said, "How did you know to poke him about oil?"

"I figured it would about be the only reason you'd wipe out a whole village. Billions of dollars in oil. Possibly billions of barrels."

"So, you're saying that Russia wants the oil for themselves?"

"Someone there does. It's either the government or our friend is a wealthy oligarch and he wants it for himself."

"If that is so, why has he got Russian Special Forces doing all his heavy lifting?"

"Because he can afford it, that's why."

Knocker seemed satisfied with that, and he sat down and leaned against the wall. Then he said, after a long pause, "We need a plan."

"Yes, we do."

The day was a drawn-out affair where we waited until darkness fell, and then we waited some more. And while we waited, the Russian and Anez left. They would keep. I would get to them eventually. The main issue was getting out. Once we were out, we would get some weapons and get the hell out of Dodge.

They weren't going to bring us food like in the movies. I mean, who does that? We were dead men. They didn't care. That plan was out. If we got the guard to come in, then we might have a show. The problem with that was with two guards, one came in, and the other stood outside the doorway with his gun pointed in.

There was only one thing to do: we waited.

And waited.

Until they came for us the following morning.

We were loaded into the back of a Linza Combat Ambulance. Our escort was two guards and a driver. For some reason, one I'll never work out, they took us about five kilometers from the base. They pulled up in a wadi and ordered us out. The two guards escorted us further along the wadi while the driver took our equipment out. I guess they were going to bury it with us.

They ordered us against the wall, ready to do their duty.

Knocker said, "Sigaretta?"

They stared at him in silence.

"For fuck's sake, you're about to shoot me and all I want is a fucking smoke."

Once more, they stood in silence until one of them shrugged and stepped forward. He took out a packet of cigarettes and offered one to Knocker.

My friend took it and held it up. "Plama?"

I stared at him, and he shrugged. "What? I don't know the word for lighter, so I asked for a flame."

The Russian stepped in closer to light the tip, which was what Knocker was waiting for. What happened next happened fast. My friend knocked the lighter aside and turned the unexpected Russian, wrapping his left arm around the startled man's throat and using him as a screen. Knocker's right hand slashed down and pulled the Russian's sidearm. It was an MP-443 Grach.

The weapon came up and he shot the second guard first. Two to the chest, taking him down hard. He then shot the guard he had hold of in the head, letting him go to drop at his feet.

We both turned our heads along the wadi and saw the stunned driver standing there, with his arms full of our equipment. He panicked, dropped it at his feet, and turned and ran.

Knocker brought the Grach up and put two more rounds in play and the Russian stumbled and fell.

I nodded. "You've been practicing."

"You never can tell when you'll need the skills," he allowed. "Or when your best friend will get you caught by Russian motherfuckers who want to kill you."

I couldn't help but smile. "At least we now have our equipment back and wheels."

Knocker nodded. "Not just any wheels. Where to now?"

My grin became a broad smile. "Damascus."

He shook his head. "Christ, you're just dead set on getting me fucking killed. Why—"

"—did you go to Damascus?" Holland asked.

"To find out what the Russians were up to. I knew in the briefing that if we were in a bind, we could meet an asset there who would help us out."

"Kind of dangerous if you know that kind of information when captured. They could torture it out of you."

I nodded. "That's why you give them what they want to hear without giving them too much," I pointed out.

"Too bad if it doesn't bloody work," Knocker said.

"My thoughts exactly," Christine Ryan said.

"As you'll see, it worked out fine."

We took the ambulance and headed toward Damascus. Before leaving, we retrieved the Russian uniforms as well, choosing to wear them just in case. They were a little small but passable.

If you look at a map, you'd think that the distance we had to travel was immense. However, it was under 400 kilometers.

We drove until noon and found a place to lay up. For us

to be out in the open in the daylight too long was dangerous. As it was, we saw a helicopter in the distance after we'd taken shelter.

Once the sun was gone, we continued our journey to the Syrian capital.

On the outskirts of the city, we stopped and ditched the ambulance, changing back into our own kit. With that done, our next move was to make contact with the MI6 asset. But first, we needed a new set of wheels.

Enter Britain's newest king of grand theft auto.

His target was a battered Hyundai parked on the street. It was unlocked and had the keys still in it. He looked at me and said, "Why would anyone just leave a half-decent vehicle like this on the street with the keys in it?"

I shrugged. "Who knows? But it's ours now. You drive."

As we would learn later, there were two reasons why someone would do such a thing. One of those reasons watched us drive away.

We reached the safehouse an hour later. I knocked on a steel door and waited. There was no answer. I knocked again and a voice said, "Yes?"

"Charlie says hello."

It was simple and effective.

"Wait there."

"Reaper, you need to take a look at this."

The door opened and a woman appeared. "Who are you?"

There was a hint of British accent among her speech. I said, "Friends in need of shelter."

She looked at us both suspiciously through large, round, dark eyes. "Come in."

Knocker said, "Not yet. Come look at this."

So we went and looked. Knocker opened the trunk, which was full of weapons. But not just weapons, explosives too. "Now we know why it had the keys still in it."

"Where did you get it?" the woman asked.

I told her and she wasn't happy.

"Get rid of it."

"Why?"

"Because if you don't, we'll have every damn terrorist in Syria coming down on top of us. Look under the back seat."

"What?" Knocker asked.

"Look under the back seat. Go on."

"Hadil, what is happening?" A man had appeared, and he carried a handgun down low.

"These idiots are trying to bring trouble to our doorstep, Omar."

"Holy shit," Knocker growled.

I looked at him and he was holding up money.

"There is loads of the stuff, Reaper. It's like a bank."

"That is exactly what it is," Hadil said. "They are all over the city. Mobile banks for terrorists. Now do you understand?"

"I think I do. Get rid of it, Knocker."

"Roger that."

He climbed into the Hyundai and drove off. Hadil turned on me and said, "I just hope it isn't too late."

They escorted me inside the safehouse. It was small but inconspicuous. There was a saferoom toward the back hidden by a cupboard. Inside were computers, weapons, and other intel equipment.

"Who are you?" Omar asked.

"We're on an op from Holly Smith," I explained. "We need to make contact with her."

"What kind of op?"

I explained what we were doing, and she nodded. "The Russians are a big influence these days. Syria is like a puppet state. I will get you a satellite phone."

When she returned, I called Holly.

She was angry. "Where the hell are you?"

"Damascus."

"What the fuck are you doing there? I ordered you into Turkey."

I explained what happened. "I'm reasonably sure that it is all about oil."

"Who is the Russian?"

"I don't know. But while I'm here, I was thinking of looking up his old friend."

"Damn it, John, that would be suicidal."

"Only if I get caught. We need the intel," I pointed out. "What's new on your end?"

"Nothing. If anyone knows anything, they're not talking. But in saying that, if this Russian is so secretive, nobody will have any intel anyway."

"Can you set us up a reception committee in Lebanon?" I asked.

"Why there?"

"Because we're going to need somewhere," I told her.

"I'll see what I can do. Put Hadil on."

I handed Hadil the sat phone, who listened for a while and then disconnected the call. She looked at me and said, "Holly wants me to make sure you don't get yourself killed. I'm thinking that might be harder than she thinks."

I grinned at her. "It's OK, I'm the sensible one. My friend, on the other hand, has a tendency to get into trouble."

At the time, I didn't know how prophetic my words actually were.

CHAPTER 9

"I THINK IT'S TIME WE TAKE A BREAK," CHRISTINE RYAN SAID. "You gentlemen get yourselves a coffee and we'll resume in twenty minutes."

Leaving the room, surprisingly without an escort, we went and found a coffee machine and mixed up some classic machine coffee which tasted like camel shit. Knocker asked, "How much do you think they really knew before we started?"

"About what?"

"About what was happening before it all kicked off."

"You mean about Sarah Nash and the Russian?"

"Yeah, fucking all of it."

"I guess we'll figure it out as we go along. I'm thinking they knew something about Sarah Nash. Maybe they were even behind it."

"Poor cow."

I sipped my coffee. "What do you make of them?"

Knocker grunted. "Typical stuck-up politician assholes. I wouldn't trust them. The only reason we're here is because they want to cover their asses, and we blew up a shit storm."

I looked down at my watch. "Time to get reamed again."

"Just what I like," Knocker said with a mirthless grin. "A good reaming by someone who knows how to do it."

We went back in and sat down at the desk. The three of them were waiting for us. Christine Ryan said, "Right. Shall we start with what happened to Mr. Jensen first? I was reading through the report, it seems interesting to me that it only got a couple of lines. Considering what it was."

Knocker left the Hyundai three blocks away. He figured that it was a good distance from the safehouse and within walking distance. He'd already unloaded our kit, so all he had was his Viking handgun.

All was fine at the start. He walked away and thought that was it. But then a vehicle showed. An SUV. It pulled over in front of him and four men climbed out. All of them were armed. Apparently, we'd been observed stealing the Hyundai.

"Who are you?" Knocker asked them.

One man stepped forward holding an AK. "I am Mustafa Samia."

Knocker raised his eyebrows. "No shit. You're that prick that cuts people's heads off?"

"Yes."

"You need to get another trademark. Other bastards are doing it too. You need something new."

One of his men stepped forward, angered by the disrespect to his leader. Knocker looked at Mustafa and said, "Tell your mate to stop or I'll put him down."

He didn't stop, Knocker shot him. Then he pointed the weapon at Mustafa and his men pointed their weapons at Knocker. "Looks to me like we've got a bit of a standoff."

"Put the weapon down," Mustafa said in a calm voice.

"Are your men willing to take a chance in making a martyr of you, Mustafa?" Knocker asked.

"Remember, it was you who started this by stealing one of our cars."

"Then how about we chalk it up to experience and forget all about it?"

"What would people think of me if I did that?" he asked Knocker.

"Then that brings us back to the question. Are they willing to take that chance?"

They stared at Knocker, waiting for their boss to say the word. But he was waiting as well. But for what? Then the reason materialized out of the darkness. Six more men, all armed.

Knocker was done and he knew it. The only chance he had of getting out of the situation he was in was three blocks away.

He lowered his weapon and grunted. "Bollocks."

An hour went by, and Knocker didn't return. I was becoming worried. My protectors could see that there was an issue. Hadil asked, "Do you want to go and look for your friend?"

"I don't know what could be keeping him."

She was about to speak again when something smashed into the front of the house. "What was that?"

Omar hurried to have a look. Moments later, he shouted, "It is a firebomb. The house—"

That was as far as he got before gunfire lashed the front of the house and its windows. Omar went down, shot in the chest. The doors would hold but were no good if they could get in through the windows or burn the place down around our ears.

Hadil hurried to Omar's side to check him while I shrugged on my body armor and opened fire with the AK-12.

Through the opening, I could see figures moving around. There were at least eight, but there would be more.

"He's dead," Hadil called out.

The fire from the bomb started to die down. Hadil said, "The outside had fire retardant on it. The flames will go out."

"What happened to the windows?" I called over to her.

"I've no idea. I've been here a month."

Suddenly the gunfire stopped, and a voice could be heard. "Mr. Jones. You need to lay your weapons down and come out."

"Is your last name Jones?" Hadil asked me. "John Jones?"

"Shit," I growled. "That's Knocker's way of telling me he is there under duress."

"This is Mustafa Samia, Mr. Jones."

That put a whole new spin on things. Mustafa Samia was bad news. "We need to get out the back before they surround the place."

"Follow me."

I took one last glance at the dead man on the floor, grabbed the rest of our kit, and followed Hadil out the rear door and into the night.

Meanwhile, Knocker was out the front, tied up and seated in an SUV. Mustafa turned to him and asked, "Where is your friend?"

"If he has any sense, trying to get the fuck out of here."

"He would abandon you?"

"I would him," Knocker said. "Outnumbered like this, I'd be heading for the hills, mate. Fuck right off, I would."

"Then I have no use for you."

"I guess not."

Mustafa dragged Knocker from the SUV and pushed him against it. I guess he didn't want to get brains all over the interior. He turned him around so he could shoot Knocker in the back of the head.

The handgun came up and Mustafa's finger started to take up the tension. Then his head exploded as I put a 5.45 caliber round into it, and he slumped to the ground.

Using the darkness of the shadows as best as I could, I picked targets and fired, shifting position when necessary. Before long, four terrorists were down, including Mustafa. This was enough to put fear into the rest of them and they started to retreat away from the deadly chaos.

I hurried out of the darkness and freed Knocker. "I was hoping you'd get the message."

"Wait," German said. "You killed a known terrorist, one wanted in many countries, just like that?"

"It was him or Knocker. Had to make a choice and follow through with it."

"But you stayed in Damascus, even after that."

"We weren't done. We had a mission to complete. If we'd run out on missions when the going got tough, we'd get nothing done."

"Some would call that foolishness."

I nodded. "I would call it commitment."

Once I had him free, we headed into the darkness once more. We were starting to hear sirens, so the best place to be was anywhere but there. I said to Hadil, "I hope you have somewhere else to go."

"Maybe, but I'm not sure I want to take you there."

We climbed into a Kia sedan and sped away from the house. Moments after we left, there was a large explosion as the timed charges went up. "They will think it was gas."

Driving through the city like a native, Hadil brought us to an apartment complex. She parked the Kia and we climbed out, leaving our weapons, apart from our handguns, in the trunk.

We went upstairs to the second floor and followed her to an apartment. It was very different to the safehouse. She opened the door and let us in. It was open plan with a sofa and a bedroom.

Hadil opened a side door that led into another apartment. This one, however, was a lot different to the one we were in. It could only be accessed through our apartment. The door into the hallway was locked and reinforced with steel. One of the rooms was converted to a communications hub, and the other had a variety of weapons in it.

"Very British," I said.

Hadil nodded. "They do not do things by halves. Now, I have to reach out to my handler. If I'm compromised, I need to get out."

Knocker suddenly realized her accent had changed. "You're from Manchester."

She gave me a disdainful look. "What? Did you think I was from fucking here?"

"I didn't know. You drive like you're local."

"Fuck you."

Knocker grinned at me. "Reaper, I think you pissed in her porridge."

"Shut up, I need to make a call."

We left her to do her thing, singed from the baking she'd just given us. I think I'd rather have been back in the firefight. Knocker said, "What now?"

"I still want to pay our friend, the minister, a visit."

"Really? Fine, whatever."

Hadil reappeared. "I've been ordered out. I'm to go with you morons to Lebanon. We can leave first thing in the morning."

I shook my head. "Nope. I still need to go and see our friend."

Hadil just stared at me. "You and him are dickheads. You really are. He's not surrounded by Syrian bodyguards. He's got Russian ones. They all have. Puppet state, remember?"

"He's the weak link," I pointed out. "If anyone will tell us what is happening, he's it."

"Shit."

"I'm sorry your friend got killed, Hadil, but—"

"My name isn't Hadil. It's Jessica. Jess for short."

"Either way, I'm sorry. But to find out what the hell is going on, we need to speak to the minister. Too many people have died already because of it. Damn it, they wiped out a whole village. We watched them do it. Then they bombed and attacked a refugee camp. Someone has answers and they need to pay for what they have done."

"Not my problem. My problem, because of you two, is staying alive."

"I need to get in touch with Holly Smith," I said to her.

She nodded to the room she had just come from. "In there."

I nodded my thanks and went into the room where I found a sat phone. Punching in a number, I looked around while waiting for Holly to pick up. "Tell me again why we weren't supplied with a sat phone?"

"Security, now, what do you want?"

"I need a UAV or a UCAV over Damascus tomorrow night."

"You're shitting me, right?" Holly sounded exasperated.

"I need some kind of cover for the op just in case things go wrong. I'm also going to give you a name. I want him in the ops room when this goes down. I'll send it to you."

"Damn it, John," she growled.

"You're a doll," I said to her in a cheerful voice.

"When?"

I told her, and she hung up. I went back out and found Knocker. "I just got us air support tomorrow night."

"We'll sure as shit need something."

Hadil/Jess reappeared. "I'm sorry for before. Listen, if you need anything, just take it."

"You got a sniper rifle?" I asked.

"No, but there is an L129A1 DMR in there somewhere."

"Can you use it?" Knocker asked.

She looked at him. "I'm good to go."

"Feel like being our lifeline?"

She shrugged. "Got nothing else to do. Not doing my nails or anything."

"Cool. You're it."

Going through the weapons cache that MI6 had set up, we took out some grenades, a couple of bricks of C4, and a smoke grenade to go with the fragmentation ones. We stuck with the AK-12s and the handguns.

For the rest of the day, we studied intel photos supplied by Holly. The minister lived a very lavish lifestyle. The grounds on which his home sat were expansive. Security cameras covered a large swathe and would need to be shut out. Ten guards, apparently of Russian persuasion. No dogs present was a bonus. Or motion sensors for that fact.

It was surrounded by a large sandstone wall with wire on top. The grounds were also covered by lights, which was another reason we needed the power gone.

Through the day, Hadil went out and came back with an SUV. She said, "We'll need it to get to Lebanon."

"Where did you steal that from?" Knocker asked.

"You don't think Mustafa is the only one with vehicles stashed around the city, do you? CIA, Mossad, German intelligence, we all do it."

"Fair enough."

When darkness finally arrived, we loaded the SUV, then drove through the streets and pulled up half a block from Anez's home. Another thing the intel told us was that the minister had a wife and two children. We'd need to do our best not to have collateral damage.

I put my earwig in and said, "Bravo, this is Reaper One. How copy?"

"Good to hear your voice, Reaper One," Sam *Slick* Swift said in my ear. "Read you, Lima Charlie."

"Hey, Slick, how's it hanging?" Knocker asked.

"Same as usual, Reaper Two. Same as usual."

"How did you go with the power, Slick?" I asked him.

"Power went down an hour ago," he replied. "It caused a little commotion, but they seem to have settled down now."

"What's the count?"

"Ten guards. Looks like the family are upstairs and the HVT is in a room on the ground floor."

"You can guide us in?"

"I'm ready, Reaper. Just like old times."

"Just like old times. Standby."

We got ready. Hadil—or Jess, or whatever her name was, maybe we'll stick with Hadil—took the DMR and headed across the street to the three-story building where she would set up on the rooftop.

Once in place, she let us know, and we moved.

"Slick, can you get that gate open?"

"I can, just say the word."

It was great to be working with him again. He was, without doubt, the best in his field. Knocker and I climbed out of the SUV and started along the street, keeping to the shadows, using our NVGs.

Once we were in position, I said into my comms, "Reaper Three, do you have the guy at the gate?"

"Copy. Target in sight."

"Bravo?"

"Clear."

I took a deep breath. "Send it, Reaper Three."

There was a suppressed crack and a grunt from the guard as the round struck home. "Open the gate, Bravo. And leave it that way."

"Roger that. Reaper, you cannot approach the house from the driveway, it's too open. Go left or right."

"Copy, Bravo."

The gate opened silently, and we entered, immediately breaking left and pressing forward. We kept close to the foliage of the garden and, at one point, walked through between some bushes. As we approached the turnaround, I paused. "Bravo?"

"Looks good, Reaper One."

I was about to move when Knocker stopped me. "Hold it. Bravo, tell me what you see?"

"It's all clear, Reaper Two."

"Three, talk to me."

"Same here. It looks all clear."

"Something is wrong, Reaper."

"What do you mean?"

"I don't know, but my Spidey senses are off the chart."

"You watch too many movies."

Knocker nodded. "Maybe. Just wait here. Let me go first."

He broke cover and ran forward, climbing the stairs and standing to one side of the doorway. Trying the doorknob, he found the door unlocked and pushed it open. Then his world exploded.

The explosion from within ripped the door off and blew Knocker backward. I let out a curse and ran forward to help him. No sooner had I broken cover when bullets started cutting through the air.

The whole thing was a trap. One we hadn't seen and walked right into.

"Wait," German interrupted. "How didn't you see it? You had eyes in the sky and an agent on overwatch as you called it."

"Nothing is foolproof. They were most likely masking their signatures."

"Is that possible?"

"Obviously it is," I said curtly.

"What the hell is going on, Slick?" I snarled into my comms.

"They were masking their signatures. They're popping up everywhere now. Get out."

I grabbed Knocker and dragged him against a sandstone wall that bordered the stairs on both sides. "Are you OK?"

"That rung my fucking bell."

"Hadil, talk to me."

"I'm doing what I can but they're everywhere."

I opened fire with my AK at some figures coming our way. One fell, but the second took cover in a garden. "Knocker, are you in the fight?"

"They knew we were coming, Reaper," Knocker said and opened fire.

"What?" I snapped, shooting at another figure.

"I don't mean we were betrayed. They just knew what we were doing." Knocker shot at another shooter who went down. "Now we're in the shit."

In the darkness, I could hear the shooters calling out to each other in Russian. I rose up to fire and almost had my head taken off by a bullet. The bastards had night vision.

"Changing," Knocker said as he reloaded a fresh magazine.

I grabbed a fragmentation grenade and pulled the pin. I threw it at a point where a cluster of shooters had made the rookie error of being grouped together. When it detonated, it killed or wounded three of them. I started firing again as more bullets cracked around us.

"Slick, I need to know what you see."

"Twenty-plus tangos are lighting up my screen, Reaper. But that's not all of it. There are six vehicles headed in your direction. They could have any amount of firepower. Two appear to be BTR-80s."

The BTR-80 was an armored personnel carrier. "Slick, do you have Hellfires on that UCAV?"

"Roger that."

"Hit that column," I snapped.

"You ordered a missile strike on foreign soil, Mr. Kane?" Christine Ryan asked me incredulously.

"I did."

"That could be constituted as an act of war."

"I did what I needed to, to survive. Besides, they weren't about to lodge a formal complaint. Not after what they did."

"Say again, Reaper?"

"Hit the damn column. If they get here, we're screwed."

"Roger that."

More bullets punched into the walls and door around their position. Knocker and I both fired at the shadows as they leaped from cover to cover. I felt a bullet target my sleeve and I was forced to drop back down behind the sandstone wall. I gathered myself and then came back up and opened fire, sighting on a target and dropping him where he stood.

Behind me, Knocker kept up a rhythmic firing. I went to shoot at another target and ran out of ammunition. I dropped out the box magazine, grabbed another, and slapped it back home.

"Frag out," Knocker said.

An explosion rocked the immediate area. I heard cries of pain as sharp shards sliced through flesh and bone. A loud explosion rocked the neighborhood as the first Hellfire from the UCAV hit its target in the column.

"The first armored vehicle is down, Reaper," Swift said.

"Good. Now get the next prick."

The incoming rounds on our position seemed to intensify. I said into my comms, "Hadil, what can you see?"

"There are more shooters closing in on your position from the north, Reaper One."

"Hold them off. We have to try to get out of here in one piece."

"I'll do my best."

Looking back at my friend, I said, "I'm going to throw smoke and then we're going to run like hell."

"Just wait a minute."

Knocker grabbed a fragmentation grenade and said, "Do it."

I grabbed the smoke grenade, pulled the pin, and tossed it out into the turnaround. It started to spurt, and a white smoke lifted into the night sky. Moments later, Knocker pulled the pin on his fragmentation grenade and threw it in the direction we were going to run. He counted down in his head, and just before it exploded, he said, "Go now."

As soon as we came to our feet, the grenade exploded, and a couple of heartbeats after that we were running toward the explosion. Bullets chased us across the yard, but we kept going.

Another explosion crashed out over the neighborhood, and I heard Swift say, "Second target is down."

Without missing a stride, I asked, "Will that hold them?"

"It should do," he replied.

"We're running for the main gate. I want you to drop another Hellfire on top of this place."

"I'll have to wait until you're clear," he replied.

"Just do it."

"Roger that. Acquiring target. Target lock. Firing… Now."

Within moments, the Hellfire smashed into the ground in front of the minister's house. A great orange mushroom cloud rose into the night sky, billowing as it climbed higher. I felt the heat of the explosion chase us toward the gate.

"Fucking hell," Knocker said. "There wasn't much room to move on that bastard."

We ran through the gate and turned to our right. As we ran along the street, I said into my comms, "Hadil, move now! Get out of there."

"On my way," she replied. "I'll meet you with the SUV."

As luck would have it, we were not on the street for long as we all arrived at the same time. Throwing our gear into the back of the vehicle, we climbed in. Moments later, we were speeding away from the site of the ambush.

Hadil asked me, "What the hell happened back there?"

"Someone set up a trap for us. No guessing for who it was."

Knocker nodded. "It had to be that bastard Russian."

"Without a doubt. Right now, we need to get out of Damascus and into Lebanon." I paused and then said, "Slick, can you hear me?"

"I have you, Reaper."

"We need the quickest route out of town."

"Roger that. Ma'am, can you hear me?"

Hadil said, "I can hear you."

"I will give you directions and have you out shortly."

"I know how to get out," she said indignantly.

Swift said, "Yes, ma'am, I'm sure you do. But I can get you out safely."

"Fine, do it."

I looked at Knocker and said, "Next time, I'll pay more attention to your Spidey senses."

CHAPTER 10

"But things didn't go quite to plan, did they?" Holland asked me. He had a smug expression on his face, and I was itching to wipe it off.

"Have you ever been out of your comfortable office?" I snapped at him.

"Do not speak to me like that, Mr. Kane."

"I'll take that as a no. Let me tell you something. I—we've fought all types across the globe, lost friends, seen them die, and these guys that we faced were some of the most resourceful we have ever seen. So how about you shut your mouth and listen."

They were starting to get to me.

"Keep going straight," Slick said over the comms as another explosion thrashed the SUV like a giant hand.

Hadil swore like a coal miner. "I thought you said you could get us out of here."

"I can't predict everything. These people are good."

The helicopter flew overhead at a height of sixty feet. It had come from nowhere, and now Slick was doing his best to keep us alive. "There is an overpass coming up. We'll try to lose him there. Stop underneath it."

Hadil came to a stop under the overpass and said, "Now what?"

"Get out of the vehicle. Take only what you need."

"Are you crazy?" Hadil asked him.

"To your left is a door. You need to go in there."

"What's in there, Slick?" I asked him as I climbed out, grabbing my kit.

"Another door. This one will lead you into a—"

The helicopter came back and hovered overhead. It was marking our position for the ground personnel that had been deployed to have their crack at us.

We went in through the door and closed it behind us. "Say again, Slick."

"It takes you into a tunnel system set up by IS when they were operating in Damascus. There are branches everywhere."

"I thought the Syrians blew all the tunnels up."

"They missed this one. Now, move. You'll lose comms for a while, but I'll be here."

"Wait," Knocker said. "Where do they go?"

"Just choose one, Doctor Who, they're like the Tardis. The corridors all lead somewhere."

"Fucking great."

For the next thirty minutes, we roamed the tunnels with no idea where we were. The system was like an underground maze which seemed to suck us deeper toward the bowels of the earth.

Then we heard a noise. Someone was following us. We stopped and I looked at Knocker. "They're not far behind us."

He took one of his few remaining fragmentation grenades and said, "Not for much bloody longer."

"What is he doing?" Hadil asked. "We need to keep moving."

"He's just setting up a little surprise."

Knocker rose. "All right, let's get out of here."

We pressed on, the NVGs a bonus because we lacked a flashlight. Minutes later, the wire was tripped, and the grenade exploded, illuminating the tunnel for a long way in each direction. Dirt and dust fell from the ceiling of the tunnel.

"That will slow them down," Knocker said.

It took another thirty minutes to break free of the tunnels. Once we were clear, we were able to reach out to Slick again. "Bravo, copy?"

"Great to hear your voice again, Reaper One. Now, where are you?"

"No idea."

"Well then, let's see if we can find you. Tell me what you see."

I ran through a few things, and he said, "Got you."

He rattled off where we were and then said, "You need to find a ride."

I looked at Hadil. "I'll ask our local banker."

"Say again."

Hadil nodded. "Follow me."

We followed her through the street. Somewhere in the distance, we could hear the helicopter's rotors beating at the air, keeping it airborne. Hadil turned left at the next intersection and froze. She ducked back and said, "Soldiers."

I leaned around and saw them standing in the middle of the street, talking. There were four of them. "Can we go around?"

"We'll have to."

We waited for them to walk the other way so they wouldn't see us cross the street. That, however, didn't happen. They came our way, heading right for us.

There was nowhere for us to hide. So, I made a judgment call. I tapped Knocker on the shoulder, and he brought up his AK-12. I followed his actions, and we waited a few heartbeats before we made our move.

We both came from cover and picked our targets, firing for deliberate effect. The Syrian soldiers dropped one at a time until all four were on the ground dead.

Knocker and I dragged them into the shadows and covered them with some rubbish we found. Then we followed Hadil further along the street until we reached another SUV.

The keys were in it. I shook my head. "I don't believe it."

She looked at me. "Anything with keys is safe. Lock it up, and it's an instant target."

She checked it before we moved. There were weapons, clothes, and money. US dollars. "Is this an MI6 vehicle?"

"CIA."

Knocker grinned. "Great, we're stealing a CIA asset."

We climbed in and I said, "Slick, we've got wheels."

"All right, let's try this again."

Pulling away from the sidewalk, we began our journey once more. We headed east toward the outskirts of Damascus, trying to avoid everything that wasn't friendly, but like I said, those who were after us were well-equipped. A lot better than your average Russian special operations.

"Reaper, I've picked up a line of four SUVs closing on you," Slick said. "Advise you turn right up ahead."

Hadil took the turn and kept going. I said, "How many Hellfires do you have left?"

"One. They only gave me four to play with."

"I guess it will have to do. Find me an open highway, Slick."

"Roger that. Turn left up ahead."

We turned left and came to an on ramp which put us onto a freeway. I looked over at Hadil and said, "Speed up until I tell you to stop."

Her foot went down, and the SUV accelerated up to

almost 100 mph. I said into my comms, "Slick, get ready with that Hellfire."

"Just say the word, Reaper One."

We traveled for a further two kilometers before I said, "Stop, side on."

Hadil braked hard and the SUV shuddered to a stop side on to the approaching traffic.

I climbed out and hurried around to the back where I found a lockbox. "I need keys."

Hadil tossed them back and I tried one in the box. It opened and I lifted the lid. Inside I found different weapons, but one in particular I was looking for. I took it out and held it up. "Good old US Army."

I was holding a detached M320 Grenade Launcher. I grabbed a grenade and loaded the weapon before putting more into my pockets. "How far out, Slick?"

"You should see them any minute, Reaper One."

We waited. Then the headlights appeared. Beside me, Knocker checked his load and made sure his weapon was ready to fire. Hadil stood on the other side of me. "Take cover."

She crouched down behind the engine block.

"Knocker, you ready for one more rodeo?"

"Always ready for a good ride, Reaper."

The speeding vehicles came closer.

"Slick, let her buck."

"Roger that. Hellfire away."

We waited.

The convoy came on.

The Hellfire hit.

The second SUV in line leaped into the air as the explosion ripped through it. The two behind it swerved wildly, both choosing separate sides to evade a collision. The lead vehicle came on, unperturbed by what had just happened.

The stock on the M320 was unfolded and I put it up to

my shoulder. Lining it up on the lead SUV, I squeezed the trigger.

Moments later, the grenade slammed into the SUV, and it stopped like it had hit a brick wall, flames shooting out of the shattered windows. It turned right, rolled a few feet, and then that was it.

While I reloaded, the shooters in the two remaining vehicles opened fire. Bullets peppered the SUV. Beside me, Knocker started to return fire. I could see his rounds punching into the vehicle on the left, so I concentrated on the one on the right.

I fired again and missed.

"Shit, Reaper, what the fuck was that?" my friend asked as I reloaded. "My dear old mother could have hit it from there, and she wears fucking Coke bottle glasses so she can see."

"Shut your hole," I shot back at him and fired again. This time, the SUV exploded, and I said, "You happy now?"

"Just as soon as you get that last bloody one."

I reloaded once more and brought up the grenade launcher. I was about to fire when the highway seemed to heave and buck from rockets fired by the damn helicopter which had returned.

We all ducked down behind the SUV as the helicopter thundered overhead. Knocker said, "That stuffed that, Reaper."

"Not yet, pal."

"What, are you going to knock it down with that thunder gun?"

"That's exactly what I aim to do."

"You are both crazy," Hadil said.

I stared at her. "Get yourself a weapon. You're in this thing now. Slick, I need to know where that helicopter is."

Beside me, Knocker and Hadil opened fire at the remaining SUV. It had stopped and the shooters decamped.

"Reaper One, your helicopter has turned and is coming back in from your two o'clock."

"Roger that."

I looked for it in the darkness and finally picked it up. Bullets hammered at the armored skin of the SUV. Finally, above the din, I heard the WHOP-WHOP-WHOP of the helicopter blades.

As I watched, it fired more missiles which fell short. Two large explosions reached into the dark Damascus sky. I ducked instinctively but forced myself back up.

Then it was there.

I fired the M320 Grenade Launcher and hit the helicopter.

With a loud bang the helicopter started spinning and crashed down onto the freeway, skidding, leaving a trail of orange sparks behind it. Then it exploded.

With that gone, it still left the remaining SUV with, by my calculations, three shooters still alive.

I had one grenade left and reloaded. "Cover me, Knocker."

He fired the rest of the magazine on full auto. While he was doing that, I stepped out and fired the last grenade. The blast was instant, and another fireball appeared. Two of the shooters were killed immediately. The third became a human candle and staggered along the blacktop before falling and squirming in pain until he died.

Then all the firing ceased. "Time to go."

Knocker checked the SUV. "It looks all good."

We climbed in. I glanced at Hadil. "Are you all right?"

"I'm fine." She appeared to be quite calm under the circumstances.

"Then let's get the hell out of here. Slick, time to go to Lebanon."

We were not long gone when Chuzhkov arrived on the scene of the battle. He pulled over, surveyed the scene, and took out an encrypted phone. "They got away."

"Follow them and kill them, Boris. Is it too much to ask?"

"I think they will head for Lebanon."

"I will task some more men to you. Maybe a Syrian army unit as well."

"Yes, sir."

"They can't get away, Boris, they know too much. Our mission here and elsewhere may depend on it."

"Yes, Comrade."

The route we chose to take from Damascus to Lebanon was about ninety kilometers, or it would have been if we'd stuck to it. Instead, we were lucky enough to be guided onto a dirt road that was twice that distance, and by dawn, we were in the middle of nowhere.

The SUV bounced over a rock before dipping into a washout hole with a loud crunch. I winced and felt pain shoot through my back from the sudden jerk. Knocker groaned and opened his eyes from where he'd been dozing in the back seat.

"I felt that one," he moaned.

The sun crept up over a ridge to the east, which thankfully put it at our back. I glanced over my shoulder and said, "He lives."

"Bloody needed that." The SUV hit another rut and lurched violently. "Remind me to have a word with Slick about this damn goat trail."

I glanced over at Hadil, who'd been driving ever since we'd left. "Pull over up here," I said.

She eased her foot off the gas pedal and pulled over,

shutting off the motor. Her shoulders slumped, her chin dropped to her chest. She was dead tired and needed the rest. I said, "Climb in the back, Hadil, Knocker will drive."

She never moved, her eyes never opened. "My name is Jess."

"If I call you Jess, will you get in the back?"

She sighed at the inconvenience of having to move but did it anyway. We all drank some water and opened rations which had been hidden under the seat. While we rested, I reached out to Slick. "How are we looking, Bravo?"

"So far, so good, Reaper One. Once you turned o,ff you lost all followers. The route you're following looks clear and it should take you to a nice quiet place to cross."

"Thanks, Slick, couldn't have done it without you."

We rested for another twenty minutes and started off again. Hadil remained asleep until we hit the first washout and began the rough rolling ride that came with the dirt road.

Then, come mid-morning, we topped a rise and Knocker slammed on the brakes before he hurriedly shoved the SUV into reverse and accelerated backward. He glanced at me and said, "Do you think they saw us?"

I shrugged. "I guess we'll find out."

CHAPTER 11

We climbed out of the SUV and walked back up the rise, keeping low off the gravel road. Using a clump of rocks for cover, we looked down at the border post, complete with guards, through the optics on our AKs.

"I count eight," Knocker said. "Looks like they've got an LMG set up on the sandbags to the left."

I swept the post from right to left and then back again. I came up with the same body count and observed the LMG. The only ones guarding the border at this point were Syrian army. "That is a bit of a bugger."

"Only if you want to get across to the other side."

Hadil joined us. "What now?"

"There is only one thing we can do," I said.

"Wait for those guys coming up behind us to catch up," Knocker replied.

I looked behind us and saw the cloud of dust in the distance. Muttering a curse, I said, "Slick, you awake?"

"I'm here, Reaper One."

"When were you going to tell us about the vehicles coming up behind us?"

"Shit," I heard him say, and then, "Yeah, sorry about that.

Looks like there are four, no, five vehicles coming your way. These guys are good."

I looked back at the border post and nodded. "I guess this is it. Everyone back in. Knocker you drive. Try not to kill anyone."

"Roger that."

"What are you going to do?" Hadil asked.

"We're going through."

I grabbed the last of the grenades from the lockbox in the rear of the SUV and loaded the launcher. I wound down the window and waited. Knocker glanced at me. "You all ready, Cisco?"

I shook my head. "Just drive."

He floored the gas pedal, and we crested the ridge at a good speed. As soon as this happened, I fired the first grenade from the launcher. Then, while it was still in the air, I reloaded. Meanwhile the first grenade hit short, more or less where I aimed. As soon as it exploded, it had the desired effect. The border guards scattered, looking for cover wherever they could find it.

I fired again and repeated my movements. This time, the round landed close enough to have dirt cascade down onto the crouching figures. I wanted them scared, not dead, so that was a good place to aim.

The third round hit almost in the same spot as the second. "Keep it flat, Knocker."

I fired my fourth and last grenade just before we reached the boom gate. I heard the rattle of dirt and stones pepper the roof of the SUV as it rained down. Then we were through. The front of the vehicle smashed the boom gate and we roared along the dirt road, a large cloud of dust obscuring us.

We were now in Lebanon, but if we thought we were relatively safe, we were wrong.

The safehouse in Beirut was a medium-sized two-floor building with a terracotta-colored façade with red trim. We were based there until MI6 could get us out that night. All we had to do was make our way to the port after midnight.

We parked the SUV farther along the block rather than outside the building, just in case. The safehouse was run by two men of Middle Eastern descent but born in London. They were both recruited out of Oxford.

We only knew them as hey you. No names were exchanged. One of them, the bigger of the two, brought us coffee. It was black, bitter, and strong. When he handed me mine, he said, "You lot have stirred up a bloody hornet's nest, that's for sure."

"Really?"

"The chatter is off the bloody scale. We're picking up Russian, Syrian, a channel here in Beirut."

I stared at him. "They have someone in Beirut?"

He nodded. "These guys, whoever they are, are very complex. They've got people everywhere. They've been talking to Moscow, Damascus, here, Germany, and London."

He had my attention with London. "What are they saying?"

He shook his head. "No idea. It's all encrypted and we can't get into it."

"Then how do you know it's about us?"

"Because after what you told us and the urgency of the transmissions, it could only be you."

"Do you know who they are talking to?"

"No, sorry. It's not the first time we've intercepted transmissions like it. We had some a while back."

"When exactly?"

He told me a date. It lined up with Sarah Nash. He said, "I do know one thing, whoever is here in Beirut is mobile."

"A search team?" I theorized.

"Could very well be."

"How close?" I asked.

"Not close enough."

"Have you ever heard word of the Russians or Syrians finding a new oil strike?"

He raised his eyebrows. "In Syria?"

"Yes."

With a shake of his head, he said, "No."

"Anything been shaken loose about a Russian ghost in the country?"

The agent looked thoughtful for a moment and again said no. "Why do you ask?"

"I'm reasonably sure that the *ghost* was behind the murder of a village for what lies beneath it."

"Oil?"

"Yes."

"I didn't know Russia was that hard up for the stuff."

"Neither did I."

"I'll see what I can dig up for you."

I nodded. "That would be great, thanks."

An hour later, he came back to me. "There is nothing at all to say that Russia is having oil problems. I even reached out to a friend in Moscow, and he knew nothing either. Mind you, all this sounded above his pay grade."

The rest of the day was spent relaxing, afforded them by the security system they had set up in and around the safehouse.

When night came, that all changed. The big guy appeared and said, "We've got visitors."

Knocker came to his feet. "Christ on a crutch. These guys just won't give the fuck up."

We went into their operations room. The other agent

was already in his body armor and kit. He pointed at the screens. "We've got these bastards out the back and these out the front."

My gaze switched between the screens. Four and six.

Something wasn't right.

I stared at the screens again. They were waiting. For what? Then it dawned.

"The rooftop. Knocker, go."

"On it, Reaper."

I turned to Hadil. "Go with him."

"You two take the front, I'll take the rear."

We thundered down the stairs and took up positions just as the intruders breached. They were all dressed in black from head to toe and armed with submachine guns. They threw flashbangs and forced us to take cover. These were followed by a hailstorm of bullets. Rounds punched into walls, and I crouched low, waiting for a lull so I could return fire.

When it came, I let loose with a long burst of automatic fire from the AK-12. I heard a cry of pain and felt satisfaction that I had at least hit something.

From upstairs, I could hear Knocker and Hadil standing their ground. While behind me, the two MI6 operatives were holding their own as well.

I was hunkered down behind the counter in the kitchen. A burst of gunfire smashed into it, lifting small tiles fixed to its top. I could feel the ceramic chips and dust settling on my hair.

Leaning around the corner of the counter I fired. Two bullets struck a shooter, and I heard a man curse in Russian.

Meanwhile, at the front, where the larger incursion was, the two MI6 guys were holding their own. They'd killed two intruders and forced the remaining ones to rethink their strategy.

Upstairs, Knocker had used his well-known unpredictability to overwhelm his opponents. He'd relied on superior fire support and dumb bravery. When they appeared, he'd hit them with a full magazine, then reloaded swiftly before opening fire again. As he did so, he pressed forward, keeping the intruders low.

As soon as he reached the head of the stairs, his magazine ran dry again, but this time, instead of reloading, Knocker grabbed his Viking handgun and shot the shooter closest to him.

The bullet hit the man in the face and hammered into his brain. A second shooter leaped to his feet. Knocker fired, and the bullet tore through his throat, creating a mural of blood over the walls.

That left two more shooters for him to deal with in his own crazy way. The first of them appeared and tried to shoot him at close range. Knocker shoved the weapon aside, which then fired, and the bullets punched into the wall.

Knocker drove the Viking into the man's groin below his body armor and fired four times. The intruder screamed and dropped to his knees. Placing the handgun against the man's forehead, he fired again.

The man flopped back, his brains running down the wall. The remaining shooter tried to do what the others had failed to. And failed as well. Another two rounds from the Viking and the fourth shooter was done.

"Are you fucking crazy?" Hadil asked him.

Knocker turned and winked at her. "You don't have to be, but it helps."

He kept going up onto the rooftop to make sure it was all clear. When he realized that it was, he began to formulate another plan. Crossing to the corner of the building where the down pipe was located, he disappeared over the side.

Hadil watched him slide down, and once he'd reached the bottom, Knocker unslung his AK and reloaded it. Then he ran around the side of the building toward the front door.

Knocker opened fire at the first shooter he saw. The man jerked spasmodically before falling to the stairs and sliding down them like a slinky.

Now caught in the crossfire, the rest of the assaulters died violently. Which left the couple I was still engaged with. However, it wasn't for long. They turned and ran after another minute or so.

I reloaded my weapon and checked the dead. They had no identification on them at all. We hurriedly checked the others, and apart from a few military tattoos, they were the same. They were Russian, former or current military, and very resourceful.

One of the MI6 guys came up to me. "We need to go. We'll head to the port and wait there. This place is rigged to catch fire. I'll trigger it before we leave. The police will be here soon."

We gathered our kits and left the house, heading for the port. There was a lot of reconstruction happening there ever since the explosion of a fireworks factory just about leveled the place. It gave us numerous places to lay up and wait.

For the next few hours nothing happened, then when it came time, we received a signal. After we reached the dock, we were picked up by a RHIB. From there we were taken out into the Med and put aboard what was classed as a research vessel and returned to London.

It would seem to me, Mr. Kane, that wherever you and Mr. Jensen go, trouble seems to follow," German said.

"We completed our mission," I pointed out. "We were assigned to find out what was happening, and we did that."

"Hardly," Christine Ryan muttered sarcastically. "Judging by the first report that was filed when you arrived back in London, there were more questions than answers."

"That was hardly our fault," Knocker growled.

"Whose idea was it to keep you working for MI6 after you returned?"

"That decision was made after the Russians tried to kill us here in England," I replied. "It kind of became personal after that."

German nodded. "Tell us about that."

"About the Russians trying to kill us?"

He nodded and held up yet another folder. "Yes, I'd like to hear it from you. Reports tend to not have all the facts."

When we first returned, we were debriefed by Holly Smith and Brian Short. It was in an interrogation room. It would have been better if it had just been Holly. But it wasn't, and right off, everyone was being rubbed the wrong way. Short took one look at us and said, "Well, well, you've returned. Tell me, what part of follow fucking orders don't you understand?"

"How about the part where fuckwits like you don't tell us the whole story before sending us into the lion's den?" Knocker snarled.

"It was need to know."

I glared at him and then at Holly. "Don't you think we needed to damn well know?"

Holly opened her mouth to speak, but Short cut her off with an abrupt, "No."

"Unfucking believable," Knocker growled. "Who sent Sarah Nash into Syria?"

"We don't know," Holly Smith said. "I'm still—"

"I did," Short stated. "It was me."

Holly gave him an incredulous look. "You, Brian?"

"That's right."

"But, why?"

"I got word that something was going on in Syria," he replied.

"What something?" I asked.

"I wasn't sure. That was why I sent Nash as a reporter."

"Well, she found what she was looking for," Knocker said. "Then they killed her and a heap of villagers with gas. Except they missed a few and had to finish the job. And us because they found out we were there."

"I had an idea that she was killed in the gas attack, but I needed to be sure."

"I found a piece of paper she'd written on, saying someone was there," I told Short. "I can only assume that it was the Russian and that she found out something about him."

Short nodded. "I had a folder come across my desk early one morning from our intel gatherers. This folder."

He held it up and then passed it over to me. I opened it to reveal a sheet of paper with two lines of writing. One said, The Gods of War. The other, Syria. I looked up. "What does this mean?"

"I don't know. I've never heard of them, which means they operate in the dark. However, something important in Syria has pulled one of them out of the shadows."

"Oil," Knocker said.

Short nodded. "But why? If Holly puts you with a sketch artist, can you give us what you can remember?"

I nodded. "I'll try."

"You've never heard of these guys before?" Knocker asked Short, making sure he was telling us the truth.

"Never. Now, tell us all you know and what happened."

We were in the debriefing for two hours telling them what we knew and answering questions. Once we were done, Short said, "All right, Holly will put you with the sketch artist, and once you've finished, you're done."

"What do you mean done?" Knocker asked.

"We don't need your services anymore."

"All right then. I can go to Plymouth and look up an old mate, drink beer, and raise hell. What about you, Reaper?"

"I might hang around London, catch up with my sister before heading back to the Med."

"Maybe I'll see you there."

"Always a bed for you."

"Great."

"Are you two quite done?" Short asked.

I shrugged.

"Good, now go away."

Once I did the stint with the sketch artist, I was done. Everything with MI6 was finished.

But it wasn't. Because the Russians were coming. And they wanted blood.

We found out later they all came in through Heathrow on a series of flights. There were thirteen of them in all. Two teams of six overseen by Boris Chuzhkov. His boss, the Russian, had dispatched them with orders to kill Knocker and myself.

Once they were through Customs, they drove straight to a place in Slough where they set up their base of operations. Chuzhkov pulled his team leaders aside and briefed them. "We have two targets. The first is here in London. This will be your target, Oleg."

Oleg Petrov nodded. "My men are ready, Boris."

Chuzhkov nodded. "Viktor, your target is in Plymouth."

Viktor Burlak looked at Chuzhkov. "Are we going to do the strikes simultaneously?"

The Russian commander nodded. "Yes. That way, we surprise them both. But be aware, these men are not like any you've hunted and killed before. They are very good and highly skilled."

"So are we," Burlak pointed out.

"Your confidence in your men is commendable but I still urge you caution. I have fought these men before. They are good. I wish they were on my team. Instead, they are to be killed."

"What did they do?" Petrov asked.

"You do not need to know. Just kill them."

"We're going to need vehicles and weapons," Burlak said.

"You will have them by the end of the day. Study the intel. You will go tomorrow night. In the morning, Viktor will leave for Plymouth. Are there any more questions?"

Oleg opened the intel folder that he'd been given. He looked at a couple of pictures and said, "This woman. Who is she?"

"It is the target's sister."

"What shall we do with her?"

"If she is there, kill her as well."

CHAPTER 12

They went after both of us at the same time. I was with Mel at her apartment. We were watching a late-night movie. A western of all things with Randolph Scott as the lead. We were snacking on popcorn and drinking beer. It had been a while since we'd seen one another, so we were making up for it before I headed home.

The movie was almost done when the power went out. Mel let out a moan and ran a hand through her dark hair. "Darn it, John, just when things were getting interesting."

She got up off the sofa and said, "I think I might have some candles in the kitchen."

"I'll get them, Mel," I said, coming to my feet.

She nodded. "Just as well, there's some light coming in from out on the street, or it would be pitch black in here."

She was right. The light was coming in from outside. I went out into the kitchen and grabbed a knife. Nothing else because I didn't have my gun. Then I went back into the living room and said, "Mel, I want you to go upstairs and climb into a closet."

"John, what's happening?"

"Just go. I'll explain later. Grab your cell and dial the police."

"You're scaring me, John."

I heard the glass in the back door go. "Now, Melanie."

She hurried away. I, on the other hand, gripped the knife handle a little tighter and crept toward the kitchen.

There were three of them pretending they were cats stalking their prey. I figured there would be that many coming in the front as well. Not the best of odds, but I could even them up some in the first few seconds.

I waited until the first reached the corner I was hiding around and stepped in front of him. Using my left hand, I forced the weapon he was carrying down and away from me. Then, with my right, I drove the point of the kitchen knife up through the skin beneath his jaw, through his mouth, and into the intruder's brain.

However, instead of letting him fall to the ground, I turned him, held him up, and grabbed his weapon with my right hand, which happened to be an MP5SD. I squeezed the trigger and started firing.

Bullets hammered through the kitchen, smashing everything they touched. One round happened to catch flesh and I heard a cry of pain. I dragged the dead man I was shielded behind around the corner with me and took shelter behind the wall.

Bullets from the kitchen punched into the soft drywall and blew through it all around me. I let the dead shooter go and pulled his weapon free. I then backpedaled along the short hallway to the living room and dropped down behind the sofa.

A shooter appeared in the doorway, and I shot him before he even realized I was there. Another one appeared, more cautious than the other, and fired immediately, raking the living room with a flurry of rounds.

They punched into the walls and the television seemed

to explode from the sudden assault. My anger rose. With these guys, yes, but more with myself for bringing such violence into my sister's home.

"Motherfucker," I ground out and fired from where I was crouched.

My bullets hammered into the wall near where the shooters were sheltered. I heard something hit the floor with a dull thud. I knew it would be one of two things, and as I flattened out on the carpet beneath me, I was hoping it was one and not the other.

I guess I was lucky. As it turned out, it wasn't fragmentation, and I could deal with the blast from the flashbang.

My ears rang, but the sofa blocked most of the burst, which figuratively smashed the room. I dragged myself back up and fired again. This time through the wall, and I heard a body hit the floor. Another shooter appeared in the doorway, and I dropped him as well with what happened to be the last bullets in the magazine.

I had no more.

I wasn't sure, but there might have been one or two shooters left. I threw the weapon on the floor and headed for the doorway which would lead me to the stairs. I took them two at a time, and just as I disappeared from the top landing into another hallway, one of the remaining shooters opened fire and sent a parting gift my way.

I went into the first room on my left. I knew Mel wouldn't be there, so she was safe for the moment. I waited beside the door jamb. They would come.

I heard one of the stairs creak, signaling the approach of at least one shooter. It squeaked again. Two shooters.

I waited. In my mind, I pictured them creeping along the hallway. Suddenly the door seemed to erupt inward as bullets smashed it to pieces. They stopped as suddenly as they started. I stepped away from the wall, launched myself at the door, and crashed through what was left of it.

My shoulder hit the shooter on the other side square in the chest. I heard him grunt in surprise. We went to the floor in a tangle of flailing arms. I hit him in the face several times and rolled away from the second shooter, taking his friend with me.

The second shooter opened fire, the bullets hammering into his friend's back. Feeling around for a handgun, I found it, removing it from the holster and aiming it at the shooter. This wasn't the movies. This was combat, and if the weapon wasn't ready to fire, the man on top of me was a moron.

I fired four shots and felt instant relief after the first. All four hit the second shooter. Three in his chest, the last tore out his throat. He stumbled backward and hit the wall before sliding down it and dying in a pool of his own blood.

That left the guy on top of me. I shot him in the head to make sure. Dislodging his dead weight, I climbed to my feet then moved to check the rest of the apartment to make sure it was all clear before heading back upstairs. "Mel?"

"In here?"

It came from the back room. She opened the door and stepped into the hallway, hurrying forward to wrap her arms around me. "Oh, god, John, who were they?"

"Men I pissed off. I'm sorry about your apartment."

"Just as long as you are all right," she said.

"I'm fine." I could hear the sirens in the background growing louder as they sped toward her address. "You're going to need a place to stay, Mel."

"I can call Cara."

I nodded. "Yeah, she'll help."

She chuckled nervously. "Just as well Raymond wasn't here, he would have totally destroyed the place."

"Oh, shit," I muttered.

"What is it?"

"They'll go after Knocker too."

They found Knocker at a pub called The Black Bull. I often wondered why a sea-faring town would have a pub named for something off the land and not the ocean. Maybe one day someone will explain it to me.

Knocker was drinking beer with his pal, Jimmy Harris. Jimmy had been a serviceman with the Regiment until he'd lost his leg early on in Afghanistan. Knocker wiped a line of condensation off the side of the beer bottle as it trickled down like it was joining the dots of water before continuing its journey.

The door opened and two men walked in, heavy coats on to keep out the wind coming in off the channel. Knocker watched them go to the bar and order a couple of beers. His gaze lingered as they paid and walked over to a table three away from where he and Jimmy sat.

"Are you listening, Bastard?"

Knocker looked at his friend. "What?"

"Didn't fucking think so."

"Sorry, Mate, something caught—"

The door opened again, and two more men walked in, halting him midsentence. They went to the bar, ordered beer, and found a table near the door. "This is even more interesting."

"What is?"

"I'll be back. Keep my beer cold."

"Knocker, what the fuck, man?"

"Just wait here and stay out of trouble."

He got up from the table and walked to the bathroom. Once inside he grabbed his cell to make a call. When there was no answer, he said, "Damn it, Reaper."

The swinging door to the bathroom squeaked as it swung open, and two men walked in. Knocker was standing at the piss trough, pretending to be relieving himself.

They stood either side of him and he said, "Water is cold."

They remained silent.

"Deep too."

Nothing.

So, he hit them. Hard.

He used his right elbow on the first man with a sudden burst of violence. With an audible crack, the jaw broke under the impact of the sickening blow. The man reeled back and hit the hard, tiled floor.

However, Knocker didn't stop there. He brought his right fist back around and hit the man on his left, who was starting to react, his hand diving under his coat for a gun.

The knuckles of Knocker's fist hit him in the throat, stopping him cold. Knocker grabbed him by the hair and slammed his face into the tiles above the urinal, smashing tiles and leaving a large splatter of blood on them.

The man's head bounced back, and he slumped to his knees. Knocker grabbed him in a head hold, jerked hard, and broke his neck.

He turned to the other man, pulled him up by his collar, hit him twice in the face, and let him fall.

Knocker flipped his coat open and found the suppressed Grach handgun. Retrieving it for himself, because it was better in his own hands, he walked out of the bathroom.

The reaction from the other two seated men was instant. They came to their feet and went for their weapons. Knocker shot the first one in the chest before aiming at the second. He fired again and hit him in the same place.

"Jesus Christ, what the fuck are you doing?" Jimmy called out.

"Call the police."

Knocker hurried outside into the parking lot. His eyes scanned the vehicles until he settled on a blue van. Grinding his teeth together, he walked toward it. Suddenly the lights came on and the van shot forward. Knocker brought up the Grach and emptied the magazine at the windscreen.

The revs fell away from the van, and it rolled past and crunched into a parked Renault. Knocker hurried up to the driver's door and wrenched it open. The driver slumped to the side and fell out onto the gravel of the parking lot.

Jimmy appeared. "Bloody hell, Knocker, what have you done?"

Knocker bent down and checked the dead man. He found the tattoo on the arm. "Fucking Russians."

"What the hell are Russians doing trying to kill you?"

His cell buzzed. He looked at the screen then answered. "Yeah?"

"You all right?"

"Fine. Can't say the same for the scousers who came after me, though."

"Yeah, me too."

"You all right?"

"Yeah."

"Mel?"

"Bit shaken. Anyway, I have to go, the police are here. They don't look too happy."

"I'll call Holly."

"Do that."

The call disconnected, and as Knocker dialed Holly, he could hear the approaching sirens in the distance growing louder.

"Someone here to see you," PC Plod said to Knocker as he opened the cell door. "Looks like a spook."

Knocker looked at his watch. "About bloody time."

He was let out of his cell and taken to an interview room

where a young man in a suit was waiting for him. "Mr. Jensen?"

"Depends," Knocker replied. "Who are you?"

"Owen Thwaites. I work for the Security Services. You want to tell me what happened?"

"Russians tried to kill me. I killed them instead."

"How could you tell they were Russians?" he asked.

"Tattoos."

"Tattoos?"

"That's right, they had tattoos that you see on Russian military. It's like being branded from different regiments, special forces, shit like that."

"Why would Russians be after you, Mr. Jensen?"

The question confused him. "Listen, Junior, who the fuck sent you?"

"I told you where I came from. I—"

"I don't care where the fuck you came from, Junior. Who…sent…you?"

"Brian Short."

"And I gather he told you nothing?"

The young agent's face flushed with embarrassment. "No."

"Don't worry, Junior, Short is an asshole at the best of times. Just get me out of here and take me to see Holly Smith."

"I was told to take you to see the boss."

"Fuck him, he can wait."

The young man gave him a wry grin. "Follow me, Mr. Jensen."

It was Holly Smith who came to me. I was also locked up in a secure cell after being taken in to Lavender Hill. When she arrived, I was sequestered in an interview room. She looked at the officer in charge when I was seated and said, "Turn off all recording devices."

"Ma'am."

She waited until it was done and said, "Jesus, John, you and your friend have created one hell of a mess."

"Not my fault," I replied. "They came after us."

"How is your sister?"

"Fine. She's gone to stay with a mutual friend."

"What are we going to do?" Holly asked.

"Bring us in and let us run with it," I replied.

"You want to come back and investigate what's happening?" she asked.

"Someone has to. Knocker and I are the best ones for it."

She hesitated for a moment, contemplating the offer. "I'll have to run it past Brian Short."

"Then do it."

She did. Knocker and I were taken to an MI6 safehouse on the outskirts of London. We stayed there with a small team of analysts, including Holly Smith. Within twenty-four hours, we had the location of where the Russians were staying.

Holly showed us a picture. "This is where they are operating from. We've got a SAS team on standby who will act as backup for you chaps."

"Us?" Knocker asked.

"That's right. You'll lead the operation. You'll meet the SAS commander on site, and he'll go through the plan with you."

"When are we going?" Knocker asked.

"Now. Good luck."

In a nondescript, unmarked white van, we were taken to the target. When we arrived, the driver led us into a building where the SAS had set up their command post. The man in charge was a major. His name was Dent. He took us into a small room they were using as a briefing room and introduced us to his two team leaders. Jackson and Merrit.

He looked at me and Knocker after the formalities were out of the way and said, "No offense, I know who you are, heard of your work, but I don't want you breaching with my teams."

"You know we're in command here, right?" Knocker reminded him.

Dent nodded. "I do, but I still don't want you with them. These men train day in and day out with each other. Throwing a—what do you Americans call it? A couple of straps—it would upset the balance of the teams."

I stared at him and nodded. "I agree."

Dent seemed surprised at what he considered a capitulation and that I didn't try to impose us upon the teams. Instead, I went on by saying, "We'll still need weapons just in case. But your people have the lead, and you call the shots with the operation."

"Thank you."

I looked at Knocker. "You got a problem with that?"

"No."

"Well, Major, go get them."

The assault in Slough was made just after dark. Two teams of SAS from the front and back. Standard. The power went off and the teams went in. And then came the explosions along with the calls for help.

Knocker and I rushed forward into the smoking building and found chaos. We were both armed with M6A2s. Most of the two SAS teams were down, taken out as soon as they entered the building. We stepped over the fallen and moved further into the building until we found the open trapdoor.

There was a tactical flashlight attached to my weapon. I shone it into the pit and saw the ladder, which dropped twenty feet straight down. It always bewildered me how tunnels were able to be dug and no one ever noticed.

I was the first down. As I descended the ladder, I said to Knocker, "If I die, make sure you cry."

"Rivers of tears, mate, rivers of tears."

The tunnel was lit and only went one way. I waited for Knocker before we started along it. After thirty feet, I found the first tripwire. It was stretched across the tunnel at shin height and attached to a claymore. These guys didn't do things by halves. I warned Knocker and stepped over it. Twenty feet further along, it turned to the left and then to the right. Fifty feet later, it went up via a ladder.

The trapdoor was rigged with explosives. I said to Knocker, "I don't suppose you have wire cutters?"

"Ah, no."

"I'll have to see what I can do."

Not one of my smarter moves.

Within moments, I'd realized my mistake and leaped from the ladder just before the IED on the trapdoor exploded. My ears rang and I coughed, but I was alive. Knocker dragged me to my feet and said, "Dickhead."

We were done. Anyone who was in the target building had gotten away.

"The SAS lost three chaps and have another three in hospital," Holly Smith informed us. "There is a good chance that one of them won't make it."

"Shit deal," I muttered.

"Very much so."

"Any idea on what happened to the scousers who were holed up there?" Knocker asked.

"We're following a couple of leads along with Five,"

Holly replied, meaning MI5. "We managed to get a photo of one of the escapees."

She passed me the photo. It was dark and grainy, but there was no mistake about who it was. "It's him. The special forces commander."

I passed the picture to Knocker. "That's him. Boris something or other."

"Boris Chuzhkov," Holly said. "He died in a plane crash two years ago along with his team. One of which has just popped up in London. This time dead for real."

"They're starting to leave a trail," I said.

"Yes, they are. All we have to do is work out where that trail leads to."

"My money is on Russia," Knocker said.

"I think that's where the smart money is," Holly agreed.

"Anything on the oil front?"

"No, although there is something interesting starting to happen behind the scenes. At first, we thought it was nothing. It might still be that. However, some members of the State Duma are dying. A car accident here, a heart attack there. One was on a ghost flight that crashed in Siberia, another died of a brain aneurysm. And there are others."

I thought for a moment. "What's the easiest way to influence a Duma?"

"Replace the ones you don't like with ones you do," Knocker opined.

"It seems an old friend has gone to Russia as well," Holly advised. "Hussain Anez."

"It looks like we're going to Moscow," I said.

"Out of the question. It is too dangerous."

I stared at Holly. "Listen, these guys murdered a whole village, killed an MI6 agent, and attacked a refugee camp. There is something in the mix that they don't want us finding out. We need to know what that is and if there is any threat to British or, worse, global security."

Holly thought for a moment. "All right. I can get you into Moscow and will have the station chief at the embassy help you out however he can. You have a couple of days to find out what you can then get out."

I nodded. "We'll take it."

"It would appear that the operation you were on was unsanctioned," Christine Ryan said.

"If it had been kicked upstairs, we were worried that it wouldn't happen."

"From the report that I have"—she picked up another folder from the large pile—"it would have been better had it not."

"If none of this had happened, then I hate to think what the outcome would have been and what you would be doing right now."

"Do you think all the deaths were worth it?"

"I guess only time will be the judge of that."

"I guess it will be. Take a break. Get a drink. We'll continue shortly."

CHAPTER 13

"DON'T WORRY, REAPER, THE BITCH IS TRYING TO GET UNDER your skin," Knocker said to me as I sipped my coffee.

"Yeah? Well, she's doing it."

"Listen, for things to get done, good people die. If they didn't, who knows what the world would be like now?"

I stood up and walked over to the trash can. I dropped what was left of my coffee into it and said, "Come on, let's head back in."

Once resettled in our chairs, we waited for the three inquisitors to be ready. German looked at us and said, "Right, let's go to the Moscow operation."

We landed at a small airport outside Moscow. MI6 had given us a new Dassault Falcon 6X. It was a dream to fly in and got us there in quick time. After we disembarked, the plane took off again and we were met by a gray-haired man named Kruger. Lance Kruger.

A black SUV took us on the journey to the embassy. "Holly Smith says I'm to give you whatever help I can."

"That would be appreciated," I said.

"What's this all about anyway?"

"We're not really sure. Have you ever heard whispers about The Gods of War?"

"I can't say that I have," Kruger replied. "Is that what this is about?"

"That is only part of it."

We drove through the streets of Moscow. Suddenly Kruger turned in his seat to ask a question as though he'd just thought of it and it was important. "Are your lives in danger?"

"Could be," I allowed. "They sent teams to England to take us off the board."

"Yeah," grunted Knocker. "They were led by a dead man."

Kruger frowned. "What do you mean?"

I told him. When I was done, I added, "He was also responsible for wiping out a village in Syria."

"This all sounds a little over the top," Kruger muttered almost to himself.

"It does. Right up to the point where it involves you."

We entered the embassy and were escorted inside. The rest of the trip I noticed that we were being followed by a BMW and a Mercedes. I said to Knocker, "Someone knows we're here."

Once inside, they showed us to our accommodation. When our kit was stowed, they showed us down into the basement where the intelligence arm was based. The setup was quite large, with ten officers going about their business. Kruger introduced us to Fiona Miller. "Fiona will help you with whatever you need. She's one of my best so don't break her."

Fiona was slim and wore a pantsuit. Her dark hair was cut to shoulder length, and she had a smattering of freckles on her face. "Come with me, gentlemen, and we'll get started."

Following her into a corner cubicle, we sat down across from her desk. "Now, Mr. Kane, Mr. Jensen—"

"No Mr.," I cut her off, correcting her. "Just Kane or Reaper. Same with Jensen."

She smiled wryly. "He's called Reaper too?"

"Knocker," he corrected her.

"Just one?"

Knocker grinned. "I see I'm going to like you. I'm sure we'll get along just fine," he replied. "Now, what do you know?"

"Whatever you are about to tell me."

I took a picture from my pocket and unfolded it. The sketch was creased, but you could tell what it was. "This guy is known as The Russian. We don't know his name or what he does. However, he was in Syria recently, where he oversaw the slaughter of a village. We think it was because there is oil beneath it."

Fiona frowned. "Never had this chap come across my desk. Bad apple, you say?"

"Very bad. Him and another guy who is dead."

"Ah yes, it is a favorite of the Russians to kill off people they need for covert operations. What is your dead chap's name?"

"Boris Chuzhkov."

She typed the name in, and a picture popped up. Fiona turned her screen and said, "This him?"

I nodded. "Yes."

"I'll see what I can find."

Fiona typed away for twenty minutes and ran everything she dug up through a printer. "When we finish with these, I'll shred them. Nothing sits out overnight."

As Knocker and I flipped through the papers that were printed, she read a bio. "It says here that Chuzhkov served in the President's Special Guard. He also served in Syria against IS and fought the rebels supporting the regime. It looks like MI6 also has him flagged for operations in Germany and another in Belgium where two former political opponents to the president of Russia were assassinated."

"Holly said that the State Duma was being thinned out," Knocker said to Fiona.

She nodded. "Over the past eighteen months, the death rate within the Duma has gone up. But it's a mix across the board."

"There must be something they have in common," I said.

"There is. They're all dead."

"We need to dig deeper," I suggested.

"What are we looking for?" Fiona asked.

"Usually if someone is cleaning house, there is a reason. In the Duma, it could be because someone wants something."

"You mean like when it comes to a vote?"

"Yes, to get a majority," I said.

"For what?"

"That is the question."

"Reaper, look at this," Knocker said.

He passed me a picture. In it was Chuzhkov and the now familiar face of the Russian. I passed it over to Fiona. "Who is the old guy?"

"I don't know. I can try to find out."

"Please. He's the man we only know as The Russian," I explained.

"Anything else?" she asked.

"He was friendly with the Syrian defense minister. Hussain Anez."

"That's interesting," Fiona replied. "It would seem that Anez is in Moscow at the moment."

"A guest of the government?" I asked.

She frowned. "As a guest of the oligarchs."

"Could our friend be one of them?" I asked.

Fiona did a quick search. "No, not that I can see."

"Then who the bloody hell is he?" Knocker growled.

"I know someone who can answer that question," I said.

"You're not coming up with some hair-brained scheme, are you, Reaper?"

I shook my head. "No. Maybe we'll just follow him around a bit and see what he does."

"Yeah, what could possibly go wrong?"

"We need some wheels," I said to Fiona. "And a couple of weapons. Grachs if you can get hold of them."

"I don't see a problem. I'll set it up, and you can start tomorrow. He's in Moscow for at least a week. Apparently, he likes the ballet."

For the rest of the day, we looked through intel pages, which told us a whole lot of nothing. That evening, Fiona ordered us a meal from the canteen. Meat, vegetables, and gravy. "I feel like I've been given my last supper," I said with a grin.

"Never can tell when your next decent meal might be, John."

"You served," I said to her. "Only someone who has been out in the field thinks like that."

"I've done my share of soldiering."

The food was good. We ate it all and then turned in for the night. The following morning, we were issued with two Grach handguns and a gray Lada which looked like it had been through the wars and come out the other side.

Fiona gave us an encrypted phone and a number to call if we needed it. After that, we were on our own. When we left the embassy, we were picked up by an FSB tail straight away. Two men in a black sedan. Knocker drove and lost them within the first few kilometers.

I recalled what we'd read in the file. Anez was meant to be having a noon-time meal with Igor Vasin. Vasin was an Oligarch who was heavily invested in the oil industry. We pulled over outside the restaurant where they were to meet.

Vasin arrived first with his bodyguards. However, he

wasn't alone. There was another man with him. Oleg Zobnin, another heavy investor in the oil industry. Only he was more of an equipment salesman.

"Interesting," I muttered.

"Well, I guess we know what the meeting is about," Knocker said.

"I'd like to know how big the oilfield beneath the desert is."

"Does it matter?" Knocker asked me.

I took up the encrypted cell. "Fiona, I need to talk to the Russian Energy Minister."

"And I'd like a charming husband who will rub my feet every night before bed and who will watch my children every day."

"Just get me within fifty feet of him and I'll take care of the rest."

"Fine. Leave it with me."

Knocker gave me one of his weird looks. "What is ticking over in that little brain of yours?"

"I want to know if he knows about the oil field or if this is as it looks. Something ticking away in the background."

"Heads up," Knocker said.

Two black SUVs pulled up, three doors opening on the first. Three men climbed out. Two bodyguards and Anez. From the second, four men alighted. A bodyguard, Chuzhkov, the Russian, and another man we didn't know. I lifted the cell which we had and took several photos of him. "Now who are you?"

The encrypted cell buzzed. It was Fiona. "Hey. The man you want to talk to is eight blocks from your current location. He is at a television studio to do an interview about some government thing. You wanted to get close to him, here's your chance. His name is Dominik Novak."

"Thanks, Fiona. Give me the address."

She reeled it off, and I said, "I'm going to send you some

photos. Could you see if you can identify the gentleman in them?"

"I'll do my best."

We left our position near the restaurant and drove to where Novak was preparing to go on air to do his interview. When we pulled up outside, I looked at the door where there was security posted. "I need a pass."

"Leave it to me," Knocker said and disappeared.

While I waited, I watched a procession of people come and go. Then Knocker reappeared with an ID tag in his hand. "Put it on back to front."

I looked at it and saw that it belonged to a female press person named Olga, who had blonde hair. I looked at him and he shrugged. "What? It's the best I could do on short notice."

I gave him my handgun and got out of the Lada. "Keep the meter running."

"Very funny."

I passed through security, which was very slack. Instead of checking me closely, they glanced to see that I had a tag while they were dealing with the woman Knocker had appropriated it from.

I entered and walked up to a wall-mounted directory. I didn't read Russian, so I did the best I could and walked through the building until I saw some wall screens. Novak was already on. I watched and listened to him, picking up every other word as he talked about coal, nuclear power, and other things like green energy.

Once he was done, I found him as he was exiting toward a hallway that led to an elevator that terminated in an underground carpark. I followed him and his bodyguard into the elevator and waited for the doors to close before I reacted.

I turned swiftly, hit the bodyguard in the throat, and then, while he was stunned, knocked him cold. Novak was horrified. I said to him, "Your man will be fine. But I needed to talk to you alone."

I hit the stop button on the elevator, and it jerked to a halt. Turning my attention back to Novak, who looked scared, I reassured him, "I'm not going to hurt you."

"Do you know who I am?" he blustered.

"I hope so, or I've just completely fucked up."

"You are an American? An assassin?"

I shook my head. "No. I wanted to ask you a question. How big is the new oil field in Syria?"

"What oil field?"

"The new one."

"There is no new oil field in Syria," he replied.

I stared at him. He believed what he was saying. I hit the button, and the elevator started to move again. The bell dinged, the doors slid open, and I was staring into the muzzle of a handgun being held by a true assassin.

Novak yelped and pulled back into the corner of the elevator. The assassin paused, seemingly shocked to be staring me in the face when he was expecting someone else. I moved swiftly, and within a couple of heartbeats, the shooter was disarmed, and I had his suppressed weapon pointed back at him.

Then I shot him in the head. Dead center. His head snapped back as though an invisible hand had smacked him on the forehead.

"Oh, my god," Novak blurted out.

The man fell forward, his body half in, half out of the elevator. I stepped out into the underground garage, looking for more threats. Not seeing any, I reentered the elevator and dragged Novak to his feet. "Get up and follow me."

"What? Why?"

"That assassin wasn't here to fucking kill me," I growled at him.

Getting to his feet, Novak hesitated as I shoved him ahead of me out into the underground garage. Almost immediately, another shooter opened fire, forcing Novak backward. Searching for the shooter, I located him standing near a concrete post. I fired three times with the suppressed handgun and jerked back.

"Why are these people trying to kill me?" Novak bleated.

"Worry about that later," I snapped back at him.

More bullets came at me and smashed into the walls around the elevator. Novak drew back even further, and we were back to where we'd started on this level. I leaned around the open doors and fired three more shots. I saw the shooter dart to his left and take cover behind a parked vehicle.

Firing twice more, I saw a window burst under the impact. The shooter returned fire with three more rounds before running even further to his left as he tried to flank my position. I turned back to Novak and said, "We need to get out of here."

"And go where?"

"If we get trapped in here, then we are screwed."

"But why are they trying to kill me?"

"I don't know, maybe you pissed someone off." My tolerance for his ramblings was limited.

I looked at his bodyguard on the floor of the elevator and bent over him, searching for a second weapon. A shoulder holster gave up its load, and I grabbed two spare magazines. Tucking the weapon into my pants, I asked, "Are you ready?"

"What do you want me to do?" Novak asked.

"When I start shooting, you run to that blue car over there near the wall."

He leaned over and saw the blue car that I was pointing at. "I don't know if I can do it."

"Put it this way, If you don't, that prick will shoot you dead."

I waited for a lull in the firing before stepping out and opening fire at the vehicle where the shooter was hiding. Calling back over my shoulder, I said, "Go now."

Novak ran out of the elevator, keeping low as he moved toward the blue car. I sidestepped three times, firing the weapon with each step. Then the magazine went dry.

I ducked down behind a red Lada, tossed the spent weapon aside, and retrieved the bodyguard's gun from my back. I came up and two rounds punched into the glass of the passenger side window, making it explode. I saw the shooter had moved once more and was now standing next to a tall concrete pillar. I fired three times, and the unsuppressed weapon roared loudly in the confined space. My ears rang at the sound.

The shooter ducked back behind the post as one of the bullets clipped it and ricocheted off into the space beyond. I ducked down and ran over to where Novak was crouched down.

"Are you all right?" I asked him.

"This is ridiculous."

I was about to say something when I caught movement from the corner of my eye. His bodyguard staggered out of the elevator. And into the open. The would-be assassin saw him as well and trained his weapon on the bodyguard's chest. He fired three times, each bullet punching into flesh. The bodyguard jerked before falling to his knees and toppling onto his side.

"Son of a bitch."

I stared at Novak. "Do not move. I'll be right back."

I leaped to my feet and started running along the row of parked vehicles. I crouched between a red and a green car, then leaped over the hood of a white one before ducking down between it and another green vehicle.

The shooter had seen my movements and opened fire. As the bullets moved along behind me, I could hear them punching through the thin exterior of each vehicle. I paused for a moment and then ran across to the next aisle. Looking up through a passenger window, I saw him move. He was going to his right. I lay on the cold concrete, peering under the vehicle where I was. I saw his feet moving and brought up the handgun.

I fired twice. The second bullet blew his ankle apart and knocked his leg out from beneath him, causing him to fall down hard. I saw his face appear. It was a mask of pain. I snapped off a shot and saw the bullet punch into his face just above the nose. His screams stopped immediately.

I leaped to my feet and jogged back to where I had left Novak. He was gone. I looked around and I saw his head bobbing up and down as he tried to sneak away through the vehicles.

"You know they're going to keep coming after you," I called after him.

I saw his movements pause and his head popped up. There was confusion on his face. "What do you mean?"

"Someone wants you dead, they're not going to stop until it happens."

"I don't understand."

"Think about this for a brief second. A lot of people in the Duma have been dying recently. More than normal. Someone is trying to add your name to that list."

His mind ticked over, trying to draw parallels to what I was saying? "Why should I believe you?"

"Because I believe the same people that are trying to kill you have been trying to kill me too. These same people slaughtered a village in Syria. Because there is an oil field beneath it."

"I keep telling you there is no oil field."

"Then someone killed a whole lot of people for no reason."

I heard screeching tires on polished concrete. I ducked down low and ran over to where Novak was. "Stay down."

The vehicle was a black BMW. It stopped in the middle of the parking garage, and two armed men got out. I grabbed Novak by the arm and guided him away from them, using the parked vehicles as cover. Along the back wall, I saw a small red box. It was a fire alarm. Moments later, the whole building was shaking as the alarms rang out.

The two assassins jumped back in the vehicle and sped away. I, on the other hand, grabbed Novak by the arm and guided him toward a fire door.

When we reached the Lada, Knocker was sitting there waiting. He took one look at Novak and said, "What the fuck is he doing here, Reaper?"

"Someone tried to kill him," I explained.

"Well, what are we meant to do with him?"

"We can't toss him back," I replied.

Knocker engaged the vehicle into gear, then drove away. I turned to Novak and said, "You've got two choices. I can turn you loose, or you can come with us. Bear in mind that if I turn you loose, someone will try to kill you again."

"I still can't understand why people are trying to kill me," Novak said.

"Maybe they just hate you," Knocker said.

I said, "Take us back to the embassy."

Two police vehicles sped past in the opposite direction, their lights flashing, sirens wailing torturously in the overcast day. What had started? Our surveillance mission was now something totally different. Word would get back that we were in Moscow. And that would make things a hell of a lot more difficult for us.

Novak was taken to the ambassador's office while Knocker and I were debriefed by Fiona Miller and Lance Kruger. The latter wasn't very happy, to say the least.

"What the fuck were you two thinking? You were meant to be observing, nothing else, and now you're in the middle of a damn shootout in Moscow, a country that will send you to fucking Siberia the first chance they get."

"Or they could just shoot us," Knocker pointed out.

"If they don't, I fucking will."

"Listen," I said. "They were trying to kill him for a reason. This wasn't about us."

"Do you think it's about the Duma?" Fiona asked.

"It has to be. Someone is killing ministers from the Duma for a reason. I say it's all tied to whoever the Russian is and whoever The Gods of War are."

Kruger nodded. "All right, just say it is. What now?"

"We talk to the weakest link," Knocker said.

"Who might that be?"

"Anez."

Kruger paused. "I just know I'm going to regret this, but all right. If you can avoid blowback on this embassy, and the British government, then do it. But if you get caught, put yourself in the same category as all those things that never bloody existed."

The door to Kruger's office opened, and a tall, slim, bald man walked in. Jeff Polter was the current ambassador in Moscow. He ignored Kruger and Fiona, choosing to focus his attention on me and Knocker. "Are you them?"

"Sir?"

"Are you the two bloody clowns who just caused an international incident?"

"If you mean by saving the Russian Energy Minister from assassination, then yes, sir."

"Don't get bloody smart with me."

"Yes, sir." Out of the corner of my eye, I could see Knocker getting ready to bite. "Should we have let him get killed, sir?"

"You should not have brought him here."

"Sure, I should have. All you have to do now is convince him to defect and you'll have a great asset."

"It's not as simple as that."

"Sure, it is. You can get his family within the hour and have him on a plane before anyone knows he's gone."

Polter looked around the room. "Would someone like to tell me what is happening?"

Kruger shook his head. "It's better you don't know."

"You're probably right." He sighed. "OK, carry on."

Once he was gone, Fiona said, "Gentlemen, tonight you go to the ballet."

CHAPTER 14

Our activities hadn't gone unnoticed once more. The Russian had called his man Chuzhkov to him. It seemed that since we figured that Anez was a weak link, the Russian had drawn the same conclusion. Now he needed to remedy it.

The black SUV eased to a stop two blocks from the Kremlin and Chuzhkov climbed in. His master was wearing a long black coat and a troubled expression. He looked at Chuzhkov and said, "We must get rid of Anez."

The former special forces man stared at his master. "Are you sure?"

"The man is a weak link in our chain. I'm sure that these people will figure it out as well. Before they can talk to him, I want him dead."

"Assassinating a foreign official on our home soil isn't going to look good, sir. Killing our own people is different. The world comes to expect it of us."

The Russian nodded. "He will be at the ballet tonight. Do it. I will take care of the rest. Now, what about Novak?"

"He got away."

A heavy silence descended over the two men. The Russian was less than impressed. "How did he get away?"

"They were there."

"Why haven't you taken care of this, Boris? They are just two men."

"Yes, sir."

"Where are they now?"

"Back at their embassy with Novak."

"Watch them. Follow them. Let me know every move they make. From now on, do nothing to them until I have said so. We need to get control of this now."

"Yes, sir."

Our plan for the ballet was simple, go in, talk to Anez, and get out. It was fluid, but we could pull it off.

I entered through the front door of the Moscow Arts Theater in the center of Moscow, passing through the security check as I went. Fiona had drawn up all the papers we needed and had gotten us tickets. I was wearing a black suit with a white button-down shirt with the top two buttons left undone.

I was really looking the part of a British Intelligence officer. James Bond, eat your heart out.

"I'm inside and making for the first floor," I said in a low voice.

"Whatever you do, John, do it quietly. The last thing we want is a blasted riot on our hands."

"Ma'am."

"Good to see you, Mr. Kane," came a soft voice in my ear from the dark-skinned woman wearing a peach-colored dress descending the stairs toward me.

I stopped halfway and she leaned in close, kissing me on the cheek. Sleight of hand passed a suppressed Grach handgun inside my coat. We parted, and the woman said in a normal voice as other patrons walked past, "I'll see you after the show."

I smiled and kept walking up the stairs. "Lovely scent you're wearing tonight, Penelope. French?"

"Of course," she replied, her voice coming through clearly in my earpiece.

"Penelope *Penny* Farthing. Twenty-eight, dark hair, soft skin, slim, attractive, and originally from Barbados. Penelope was an MI6 officer from the embassy. We needed an extra, and she volunteered to come on board. Even she deserved to be in a Bond film with a name like that."

I topped the stairs and turned to my left, walking along the rear of the private boxes until reaching the fourth one. I opened the door and entered. There was one other person inside. Sitting beside Knocker, I asked, "Have I missed much?"

Knocker turned to look at me. "On the contrary, Reaper, we're just getting started."

Looking out across the space toward the private box on the opposite side, I took in the three couples seated in the luxury box. One of those being the Syrian defense minister.

"Anez," Knocker said. "All we have to do now is wait for him to do something and go from there."

"Good looking too," Penny said over the comms.

I looked to the left of the minister's box and saw her entering. She was the only one there. I said, "I think he looks like a cow's bloody rectum."

"Jealous?"

I snorted. "Not hardly."

"Focus," Fiona said.

Intel hadn't come to light about the assassination attempt to be carried out on Anez. However, it didn't take long before Fiona picked up something she didn't like.

"Gentlemen and lady, I have Chuzhkov entering the rear

of the building with a duffel. I do not like the look of it at all."

"Make the call, Fiona," I said.

"It has assassination written all over it."

"Then we'd better stop it."

My face turned grim, and I looked up, ignoring the sudden sound of the orchestra below and the trills of a soprano opera singer just getting started. Above the stage and the crowd was a maze of gantries and ropes beyond the large bright lights. "He's going up there."

I came to my feet and walked out of the box. In my ear, I heard Fiona say, "For God's sake, be discreet, John."

Chuzhkov placed the duffel beside him on the gantry and reached inside, retrieved the specially made sniper rifle piece by piece, and clipped it together, the last bit of the puzzle being the suppressor. He took off his burgundy coat and hung it neatly over the handrail.

Below him, the orchestra began to crescendo, and a woman's melodic voice floated up, enveloping the assassin in its embrace.

Boris loved the power of opera. He suddenly felt the emotion of the opening song and tears welled in his eyes. He wiped at them and brought the rifle up to his shoulder, sweeping the boxes below as he sought his target.

There. Anez sat with his wife. The rifle moved again and settled on the coffee-colored young woman in the box next to them. "Hello, what do we have here?"

Chuzhkov flicked through his photographic memory and came up with a name. "Penny Farthing."

The rifle moved again as the former special forces commander searched for me.

The sights came back to the minister's box. His wife was leaning across him, talking to the man on his left.

Chuzhkov waited.

Waited.

Waited.

And then fired.

I made my way upward into the gantries and ropes beyond the prying eyes of the audience below. It was as though I was operating in space where nothing could be seen.

Holding onto a handrail, I walked across the cavernous void below. Changing paths, I worked my way toward the only place I thought that Chuzhkov could be.

But he wasn't there. I frowned and looked around the shadows for the killer. "I can't see a bloody thing up here. Anything, Penny?"

"Nothing yet, John."

"He's here somewhere." Then came the dreaded sound of the suppressed sniper rifle. "Ah, fuck!"

Dropping my glance directly beneath me, I saw the figure. Without thinking, I jumped over the gantry rail and plummeted toward the assassin.

Landing directly behind the killer, I knocked him forward onto his face on the steel catwalk. He lost his grip on his rifle, and it spilled over the side, lost into the backstage abyss below.

Chuzhkov turned and looked at me. With a snarl, he lashed out with a foot, kicking me in the head.

I grunted, stunned momentarily by the blow.

The former special forces commander started to climb to his feet, but I grabbed his leg. "Not so fast, asshole."

He swore at me. Chuzhkov grabbed the gantry rail and kicked out with his free foot. The force of the blow drove me to the side with a heavy grunt of pain and I found myself suddenly falling through emptiness.

I hit the gantry below solidly, the air rushing from my lungs. With a groan, I dragged myself to my feet and started a shambling run along the hanging platform.

Below me, the orchestra had stopped playing, and I realized that Fiona was shouting in my ear, "What the bloody hell have you done, John? Speak to me, blast your eyes."

Ignoring the demand, I climbed the stairs up to the next level. Stopping halfway along, I saw Chuzhkov on a lower level, heading toward another set of stairs that would take him down.

I looked around for a quicker way, shook my head, and said, "I just know I'm going to regret this."

Reaching up, I grabbed one of the ropes that would normally hold a backdrop. Then, taking a firm grip, I leaped over the rail and swung through the mess of rigging like Tarzan.

I hit hard when I landed, adding to my already painful list of woes. At the end of the gantry I now stood on, I saw Chuzhkov about to disappear. Taking out the suppressed Grach, I fired three shots at the retreating figure.

All of them missed.

"Damn it, he's getting away."

"Well get after him, man," Fiona said. "Raymond, keep an eye on Anez."

I ran along the gantry, chasing after the Russian. He was about to leap down the stairs when a voice came through my comms. "John, he shot me."

I stopped. "Penny?"

"Help me."

"Shit, hang on."

"Kane, get after Chuzhkov," Fiona growled. "He is a key."

"John?"

"Hang on, Penny," I said reassuringly and turned back along the gantry. "Knocker, he's headed for the back door."

"On it, Reaper."

Halfway, I stopped and peered downward, searching for Penelope. Then I saw her. She was sitting in her seat, her peach-colored dress now stained with a large blossom of blood. "Christ."

"Kane, damn you." This time it was Kruger.

I ignored him too and reached for another rope. "Twice in one night. This is some kind of record. Who needs culture anyway?"

Then I leaped into oblivion.

As I swung above the audience below, the danger of what I was doing sent a massive wave of euphoria coursing through my body. Which lasted mere seconds when I realized that I was coming in too low and was about to hit the wall of the box below the balcony.

"Oh, Christ," I cried helplessly and braced for impact.

I hit solidly, and for the second time in less than an hour, the air was forced from my lungs. I let go of the rope and grabbed at the detailed tapestry hanging over the balcony edge.

I felt it tear, and I dropped a few feet before stopping. I looked down and saw the mass of seats below. If I fell, I'd land among them. Possibly die, at best be crippled.

"Bet you never thought this would happen when you came to work this morning," I muttered to myself. "Shit."

I started climbing hand over hand and reached the balcony edge, hauling myself over to find Penelope still slumped in her seat.

Crouching beside her, I examined the wound. "John?"

"Yeah, it's me. You silly woman, what the bloody hell did you want to get shot for?"

"I thought it might—might get your attention."

I pressed against the wound to stanch the bleeding. "Fiona, I need medics here right now."

"They're on their way."

I stared at Penelope. "Tell them to hurry. Knocker, where are you?"

"Yeah, I'm a little busy right now," came the reply.

There was a shuffle of movement and a voice said, "Say goodbye to your friend, Mr. Kane."

"How did Mr. Jensen get captured?" Christine Ryan asked.

"It was my own stupid fault," Knocker replied.

"That part wasn't in the reports I have read," she replied.

The woman was trying to make him look incompetent. "Ma'am, when things start to become fluid on a mission, things can change in an instant. When I made the call for Ray to go after Chuzhkov, things were on a slide. Decisions were made on the fly, and we had an operative down. It isn't surprising that he was captured."

"How did you get him back?"

"We have one of them in our care," Chuzhkov told the Russian over the encrypted cell. "What do you want us to do with him?"

"Have him sent to Chistilishche," the Russian said. "They will look for the other one, find him, and send our friend to get him. Then we can kill them both."

Chistilishche was a penal camp inside the Arctic Circle. It was one of the toughest prisons in Russia. It was home to murderers, political prisoners, former soldiers, and anyone else deemed worthy of being placed there. Translated, the camp lived up to its name of Purgatory.

"What about Anez?"

"You were right, they were there. We will have to use the other backup we discussed."

"I figured as much. But don't worry, they will never talk to him."

"I will transfer our passenger myself."

"Good. I have the next part of the operation to worry about."

"Yes, sir."

"Thank you, Boris."

"She's going to be fine," Fiona said to me. "She lost a lot of blood, but luckily the bullet missed anything vital."

"What about the Syrian?" I asked.

"Intel has him on the way to the airport heading home." She paused then said, "But why shoot Penny?"

"Send us a message, I suppose. Do we have anything on Knocker?" I asked.

"Nothing yet. Only that he walked into the situation and was put in a van."

"We need to find him before they kill him."

"Do you think they might have something else planned for him?" Fiona said. "I mean, if they were going to kill him, they would have already done it."

What she said made sense. I nodded. "They want me to find him so they can finish me as well."

"But where do you think they might take him?"

"Somewhere out of the way," I replied. "A place where only hell exists."

Fiona's eyes widened. "A penal camp."

"How many do they have?"

"Six."

"So, which one of the six are they going to take him to? Which is the worst of the worst?"

Meanwhile, the Russian kept his plan rolling forward. While we were trying to work out where Knocker was, he was involved in a very important meeting that would affect his country.

Dmitri Volodin was the chairman of the State Duma and an ally of the Russian. They were currently having coffee together in a small café in a back alley perfect for clandestine meetings. The Russian sipped his strong black coffee while Volodin updated him on the Duma's process. We need two more votes, and then we can proceed. Novak will be a problem—"

"No, he won't."

"Why?"

"He is currently hiding in the British embassy because someone tried to kill him. What you need to do is convince everyone he has defected. Replace him, get one more vote, and then we can impeach. With the president gone, nothing will stop us."

"I cannot believe we are almost there."

"Everything is just about in place. There are a few more things, but it won't be long. Then no one can stop us."

Later that afternoon, Fiona came and found me while I was recuperating from my bruising encounter with Chuzhkov. It was all I could do. She had a worried expression on her face.

"What is it?" I asked her. "Knocker?"

She shook her head. "Hussain Anez's plane has gone down over the Caspian Sea."

"Shit. Do we know how?"

Fiona shrugged. "No, but you can bet that it didn't just crash."

"There goes that," I said.

Fiona held up a photo and passed it over to me. "This is a satellite photo from the village that was massacred."

I looked it over. Gone were the houses and buildings, all replaced by machinery. "They're not wasting any time. Did Novak look at pictures of the Russian?"

"Yes, he knows nothing."

"Someone does. Something big is happening and we need to find out what it is."

CHAPTER 15

Transport was a mix of plane, helicopter, and truck. Knocker was looking across to the bench seat opposite him where three other prisoners sat and knew from experience that at least two of them would be dead before the week was out.

One of them, the thickset man with a scar on his right cheek, looked at him and snarled in Russian, "What the fuck are you looking at?"

To the man's surprise, Knocker responded in Russian himself, "An ugly cunt."

The prisoner lurched forward and stopped suddenly when Knocker hit him in the face, breaking his nose and knocking him silly.

"Hey you, stop!" one of the guards shouted. He looked at the blood dampening scarface's clothing and shook his head. "Stupid asshole."

Knocker felt the cold from outside filter beneath his thick coat. Scarface wiped the blood from his face and glared at the man who'd broken his nose. "You are fucking dead, Englishman."

Knocker smiled at him and pretended to stroke his cock. "Wanker."

Beside Scarface, one of the other prisoners chuckled. Suddenly Scarface was onto him, pounding at him with both fists. The two guards let out curses and separated the pair. Now there were two prisoners bleeding in the back of the truck.

The vehicle lurched as it hit a hole in the icy road. The rear end slid sideways, and Knocker felt the driver take his foot off the gas pedal to let it slow.

The truck had been traveling for the past six hours through the nasty weather. Originally, a helicopter would have flown them the rest of the way, but the storm had forced it to terminate well short of its destination.

Five prisoners had begun the journey. When an older prisoner, thin-built and sickly-looking, had deteriorated, he'd been left to die beside the road under the orders of Chuzhkov shortly after crossing the Arctic Circle. He never made a sound, just accepted his fate. It was as though he welcomed death and knew it was preferable to what the other prisoners were going to live through.

An hour later, the truck slowed and turned left. It gathered speed once more before slowing again, then stopping. It sat idling and Knocker could hear the wind above the motor. He heard voices, and then gears grated and the truck lurched forward once more before stopping.

They were forced from the back of the truck into the snow that swirled around them, buffeted by the wind. They were just in time to watch the large steel gates swing shut with a loud boom.

A second set of steel gates swung inward, revealing an open yard filled with men dressed in heavy coats. Some were walking. Others just stood there and watched the new arrivals.

"This is your new home," Chuzhkov said as he stepped

up beside Knocker. "On average, new people last three days."

Knocker turned his head and said, "Come back next week and I'll still be here."

"I doubt it. See, the prisoners run the camp. The guards keep them in and feed them." He nodded at a group of men on the other side of the outdoor compound. "Soslan Kutepov. Russian Mafia."

"Great, we should be fine friends."

"There are different factions, all at war with each other vying for total control of Chistilishche."

"Sounds like fun."

"Goodbye, Mr. Jensen."

Knocker smiled at him. "Fuck you."

Then he was gone, and the gates closed, and Knocker said, "Why do I always end up in these fucking places?"

"Hello, Meat."

Knocker turned and saw a large bear of a man standing three feet from him, bare-chested in the freezing cold, a prison tattoo across his chest saying: *You are my bitch!* in Russian.

The big prisoner grinned, revealing blackened teeth as he undid his stained pants and let them fall to his ankles. He grabbed his crotch and said, "You are my bitch."

Then Knocker kicked him in the balls.

The big man's face changed color as he slowly sank to his knees. Knocker stepped in close and hit him four times in the face with his elbow. The second blow broke his jaw, the next two made sure he wasn't getting up anytime soon. One thing about my friend, when it came to tight spaces, he was good—or just crazy.

The big Russian toppled onto his side in the snow. Knocker looked up and saw everyone was looking at him. Then came a roar of anger and a thinner man standing about six feet came running at him, a large homemade blade in his right hand.

Once he was close enough, Knocker reached up and grabbed the knife-wielding arm in a vice-like grip. He pulled it down and twisted savagely. The man's momentum carried him forward so that he ran onto the blade under his own power.

Knifeman stopped suddenly, eyes wide, shock etched deep in his face. He coughed once, blood running from his mouth, and then he fell backward and lay beside his big friend, knife still embedded.

Knocker looked up just in time to see the wall of prisoners coming at him.

Knocker spat blood into the snow at his feet. The fight had lasted a couple of minutes, which seemed like a lifetime. In that short space, he'd laid out four more men before being overwhelmed.

He'd taken numerous blows to the body and a couple to the face. Then it was stopped by the booming voice of Mikhail Shatov. A path had cleared, and the former Russian officer stood there like a tree. "You have skills."

"Yeah, you want to fucking try me?"

The man grinned. "English. We don't often get English here."

"Really? What happened to the last one?"

"He was killed by Kola's men."

"Who is Kola?"

"Edvin Kola, Albanian Mafia."

"Wonderful. Who are you?"

"Mikhail Shatov. What is your name, English?" Shatov asked.

"Just call me Raymond."

"What did you do, Raymond, for you to be sent to Purgatory?"

"Pissed off the wrong person."

"Who might that have been?"

Knocker shook his head. "That's the funny thing about this mess. I don't actually know his name."

He slapped Knocker on the shoulder. "Come inside. The cold out here is shit."

As they started sauntering toward the main block of the prison, Knocker asked, "Who was the big guy?"

"One of Soslan's men. It was a test."

"He won't be testing anyone else for a while."

Shatov nodded. "You need to watch your back from now on, my friend. It has got a big target on it."

He escorted Knocker into the dining hall, where a drum burned rubbish and kept the place warm. They sat at a table and continued their conversation. "Why are you here, Mikhail?"

"I was a general in Russian army. Long story. I will not bore you with it."

"We're not going anywhere."

Shatov nodded. "OK. When I came here, I was general. Everyone calls me colonel."

Knocker waited for more, but nothing was forthcoming. "Is that it?"

"Yes."

"I thought you said it was a long story."

He shrugged again. "For me, it is."

"Bollocks."

Shatov frowned. "What is bollocks?"

"Balls."

"Ah, yes."

"So, how did you get here, General?"

Shatov smiled. "I like you."

"What's not to like?"

"I was part of something and didn't want to be part of it anymore. Now, here I am. For five years I have been here."

"Long time."

"Very."

"Why did you keep them from killing me?" Knocker asked.

"News."

"What?"

"You are new here. You will have news from outside."

Knocker raised his eyebrows. "Really?"

"Hey, five years."

"Fine. But you do something for me," Knocker said.

"What?"

"Watch my back until my friend arrives."

Shatov nodded. "Fine. What happens then?"

"When?"

"When your friend arrives?"

"I'll be leaving."

Shatov laughed out loud. "Now I know you are funny."

"Yeah, funny as fuck."

Shatov looked at his watch. "Come, it is eat time."

Knocker indicated the room. "Aren't we in the dining hall?"

"Yes."

"But—"

"Come, Raymond."

They went back outside just in time to see the dump truck back in through the steel gates. It jerked to a halt and started to lift the bed. Moments later, the gate at the back swung and a bloody mess slid out. Shatov nudged him. "Come, get some food."

The smell hit him before he even got close. Men rushed forward and dug through the mountain of meat to find something edible. Knocker stared in disgust at the throng of prisoners.

It was like a sale day at one of the big London department stores. Knocker felt his guts lurch as he watched them dig through the mess. When Shatov returned, he had blood up to his elbows. "We have a hierarchy in here except when it comes to food. Every man for himself. I grabbed you something."

Knocker stared at the lump of meat and shook his head. "I don't think I'm that hungry."

"You will be."

Suddenly a fight broke out between two of the prisoners. Shouts could be heard as one of them pulled a homemade knife. Moments later, the second man was reeling away with the knife buried deep in his chest.

Knocker saw that Shatov had a concerned look on his face. "A friend of yours?"

"He is one of my men."

"I thought you were a big man in here, General."

The Russian ignored the comment and nodded at another man. This one stepped forward behind the killer and ran his hand across the man's throat. What Knocker didn't see was the small razor-sharp blade the man was holding.

The killer staggered around as blood spilled from the slash in his throat. He dropped to his knees and died beside Shatov's man.

"What is the point of all this?" Christine Ryan asked impatiently.

"If you allow me to continue, you will eventually find out," I said.

"Let him continue, Christine," German said. "I want to hear more about Shatov."

"Oh, very well."

"That'll do it," Knocker said.

"A killing does not go without revenge," Shatov said.

"So I can expect the same?" Knocker asked.

"I told you I would watch over you until your friend arrives. And I—"

He stopped speaking when Edvin Kola stepped out of the crush with three of his men flanking him. Kola was a thin man but looked ugly mean. He had tattoos on his neck, and Knocker guessed they would adorn all of his body.

"I guess he wants to talk to you," Knocker said.

"He does. I will meet you inside." He shoved the meat he held at Knocker and said, "Take this."

Screwing up his nose, Knocker took the rancid meat. "Thanks."

Once cooked, the meat wasn't too bad. Juice ran down Shatov's chin as he ate like a pig. Knocker joined him and they were flanked by five of Shatov's men. The meat had been cooked over a large fire which made it just like an outdoor barbecue.

"What happened with Kola?" Knocker asked.

"He wants revenge for his man being killed," Shatov explained.

"So he wants revenge for you getting revenge for his man killing one of yours?"

"Yes."

"Kind of a vicious circle, isn't it?"

"No. The two chosen men will fight, and that will be the end of it."

"Prison rules, huh?"

"Yes. Now, Raymond, tell me, what news from the outside?"

Knocker nodded. "What do you want to know?"

Shatov smiled. "Everything. I have a lot of time."

"The energy minister is going to defect," Knocker said.

"Who is energy minister?" the Russian demanded.

"A chap called Novak."

"Dominik Novak?"

"Yes, that's him," Knocker replied.

"Pah, a spineless coward."

"Well, someone wanted him dead. They tried to kill him, but me and my friend stopped them."

"Who tried to kill him?"

"A Russian. I don't know his name. Just one of many."

"There have been others?" Shatov asked.

"Quite a few. All made to look like accidents or natural causes."

Shatov nodded thoughtfully. "What else?"

"There was a new oil field found in Syria," Knocker said. "Bastards killed a village to get to it."

"Who did?" Shatov asked. His face had grown serious, and Knocker hadn't missed it.

"It was a Russian guy. The same one who was behind trying to kill Novak."

"Bastard."

"Say, do you know anything about a group called The Gods of War?"

"Never heard of them," Shatov said. He was lying, but Knocker knew to leave it alone.

He took another bite from the meat, which was now cold, but figured he needed it. He looked back across .at Shatov, who had gone quiet, his cheerful demeanor gone. Shatov knew something, but the question was, what?

Chuzhkov wasn't happy about the call he got from the Russian. He'd just found out that after five years, an old friend was still alive and could pose a threat—even if it was remote—and he wanted him gone. That meant Chuzhkov had to make it happen. Especially now that they had the numbers to win the vote in the Duma.

But his old friend knew everything they would do. He'd been part of their organization until he had faltered, and they had been forced to get rid of him. But he was still alive. That meant he was a threat. And threats needed to be neutralized.

This was why Chuzhkov was back at Purgatory, standing in a small room facing one of the prisoners. "Can you do it?"

The man nodded. "Yes. But, when it is done, you must get me out."

"I can do that," Chuzhkov lied.

"Then I will do it."

CHAPTER 16

I WAS LOOKING THROUGH INTEL FILES WHEN TWO LOTS OF news came in. Fiona broke both to me. The first came as a surprise, the second was good news.

"The State Duma is impeaching their president," she said excitedly.

"They what?"

"That's right, they're getting rid of Kuzmin."

I stared at her, my mind whirling. "Who are they going to replace him with?"

"Don't know."

"That has to be what they were playing toward," I said. "But why? What is their endgame?"

"I have no idea. But we now know where Raymond is. We've tracked him down."

A wave of relief swept over me. It proved to be short-lived. Especially when I found out where he was. "Where is he?"

"Purgatory."

"No, really, where is he?"

Fiona nodded. "Purgatory. It is a prison above the Arctic Circle. They send prisoners there to die."

"How the hell do we get him out from there?"

Her face grew grim. "We don't. You do."

"Be fucked."

"We will give you all the help we can, but ultimately, you will be on your own."

I hung my head as my mind raced into planning mode. "I need schematics of the prison."

"I think we can manage that."

"I'll also need insertion and a snowcat."

"Yes."

"Weapons and a first aid kit. Extra ammunition."

"What kind of weapons do you want?" Fiona asked.

"MP5SDs," I replied. "Two of them. Stun grenades, fragmentation grenades, I'll need body armor as well. Everything will need to go into a pack I can carry."

"I can organize that."

Knocker sat on his bed and listened to the sounds in the dark. Somewhere in the middle distance, it sounded like a prisoner was being tortured by another. The crazy cackle of one prisoner echoed from a lower floor, signaling the state of his mind. No one would come. The guards just manned the perimeter. Making sure no one got out. No one was ever crazy enough to try and break in.

Lighting was dim. The only power source was a small generator barely sufficient to supply the prison. What there was made it look like the prison was in permanent brownout.

"Are you awake, Raymond?" Shatov asked.

"Who sleeps in this shit hole, General?" Knocker said in a quiet voice.

The Russian appeared in the doorway. "I would talk to you."

"Sure, come on in."

The general entered, leaving his men outside. He sat next to Knocker and said, "When your friend comes, I want to go with you."

Knocker was surprised at the suggestion. "Why? I mean, I know why you'd want to get out of here, but why?"

"I have something you want, and for that information, I am wanting payment. That payment is to get me out of here and to Moscow."

"What information?" Knocker asked.

"About those you seek."

"The Gods of War?"

"Yes."

"What do you know, Shatov?" His voice was harsh now.

"Get me out, Raymond, and I will tell you."

Knocker didn't know whether to believe him or not. "You'd better not be screwing with me, General, or I'll bury you up here."

"Do not threaten me, Englishman," Shatov growled. "Just remember who you are talking to."

"All right. When my friend comes, we'll take you with us."

"You will not be sorry."

He left then, just got up and walked out, leaving Knocker to his thoughts.

Knocker lay back on the bed, his butt sinking so low it felt as though he was almost bent in half. The screaming had stopped, but the smell of the prison remained. The smell of death.

He thought about Shatov for a while, trying to guess what the former general knew. He was just about asleep when he sensed someone was there. He opened his eyes and saw the outline of a prisoner standing in the doorway of the cell.

Knocker sprang to his feet, ready just in case the prisoner was there for violence. He said, "What the fuck do you want?"

"I want to talk to you."

"Who are you?"

"Soslan Kutepov," the Russian said. He stepped forward and dark shadow gave way to the dull orange of the light. It shone on Kutepov's face and Knocker could see that it was him. "Can you see me better now, Englishman?"

"Say your piece," Knocker replied. "I need to get some sleep."

"I am not here to kill you. What if I told you I can get you out of here," he said.

Did this idiot think he was stupid? If he could get Knocker out, it stood to reason that he should have been able to get out himself. "How?" Knocker asked.

"It does not matter how. What matters is what you have to do to win my help."

"And what might that be?"

"Kill Shatov."

"Really? That's it? Just like that?"

"You have gotten close to him. It would be easy for you to do it."

"It would be easy to get myself killed trying. Why can't you do it?" Knocker asked.

"Like I said, it is easy for you to get close to him."

"And you can get me out?"

"As soon as it is done," Kutepov said.

"What about the guards?"

"You ask too many questions."

"Asking questions keeps you alive," Knocker replied.

"Will you do it or not?"

"Can I think about it? Size it up?"

"Do not think too long, my new friend. The clock is ticking."

"Why, are you going somewhere?"

Kutepov stood up. "Yes, to bed."

He walked out of the cell and Knocker moved to stand in the doorway. He looked left and right and saw Shatov's man standing at the rail, looking down into the void below. *So much for fucking loyalty.*

The man turned and looked at Knocker and just shrugged. Then he turned back to the rail. Knocker went inside and lay down once more.

The next disturbance roused him from sleep. He woke up with a start, another figure in his jail cell. This one, however, was coming toward him with a homemade knife in their hand.

Knocker powered off the bed, all vestiges of sleep gone. The knife slashed down and, by some miracle, missed. Knocker leaped to the left and circled out of the corner. The prisoner hissed with displeasure and came at him again. A straight left from Knocker pulled him up short, forcing the attacker to gather himself again.

With a grunt of anger, he came at Knocker once more. Knocker sidestepped and hit him behind the ear, causing him to fall to his knees. "How did you like that, motherfucker?"

The knife was still in his hand as he came to his feet. Whoever the man was, his skill with a knife was pretty shit. He resembled a bull at a gate instead of the skilled ballet dancer type that it took to be a competent knife fighter.

The bull charged again. This time, Knocker caught up his arm, twisted it, and brought it down over his knee. It was like snapping a dry twig. The man screamed in pain and dropped the knife.

Next, Knocker grabbed him by the hair and dragged him furiously toward the cell doorway. Then, before the killer knew what was happening, he was going over the rail.

He screamed as he fell, his arms waving as though they

would arrest his death-fall like the wings of a bird. The crunch that followed was sickening.

Knocker didn't bother looking as he sucked in deep breaths. A voice said, "See, it is a dangerous place to be, Englishman. Think about my offer."

Knocker looked at Kutepov. This time he had a couple of bodyguards with him. "I'll do that. In the meantime, you might want to teach your men to fly."

Kutepov disappeared and it wasn't long before Shatov appeared. "What the fuck happened to your man?" Knocker asked.

The Russian shook his head. "I will look into it. Is there anything you would like to tell me, Raymond?"

Knocker shook his head. "Not at this time."

"Then watch your back."

Knocker went back to his bunk. He never slept.

The fight the following day to settle the debt of honor was brutal hand-to-hand combat. No weapons, just fists, feet, and teeth. Both men were evenly matched in height and size. It happened in the open yard under a curtain of snow from a passing storm.

A large circle was formed around the combatants. It was like the circus had come to town. Complete with cheerleaders.

Knocker watched from where he stood next to Shatov. The general remained silent, and Knocker contemplated how easy it would be to kill the man right at that point in time. He looked across the circle at Kutepov, who sensed his stare and returned it. Knocker knew he was responsible for what had happened the previous night.

Meanwhile the two combatants fought. Shatov's man

looked strong, more than capable, while Kola's man was agile and quick.

They traded blows and blood flowed. The Shatov man lost a finger when it strayed too close to his opponent's mouth and he bit down hard on it. The Shatov man growled in pain, blood spurting from his now severed finger.

He headbutted his opponent and opened a gash above the Kola man's brow. Blood poured down the man's face as he staggered back. Kola's man gathered his feet beneath him and shook his shaggy head. He shouted a curse at the Shatov man and charged.

He hit him in the chest, and Shatov's man staggered backward. Kola's man went low, and his hand caught his opponent by the testicles. He squeezed hard, virtually crushing them in his grip. Shatov's man howled in pain.

Kola's man had become careless once again as his head was close to Shatov's man. Blunt teeth gnashed together, catching the man's ear. Shatov's fighter jerked his head back, and with it came most of his opponent's ear.

The elicited scream peaked above the cheering and was worse than when the finger had been severed from Shatov's man. The ear was spat out to land bloodily in the snow, only to be trodden on by both fighters.

Knocker winced. "That had to hurt."

Blood poured down the side of the Kola man's face like a red sheet as it mixed with sweat. The pain only served to make him more determined to kill his opponent.

He launched into a flurry of blows. Some landed, others missed, but the onslaught had the desired effect. The Shatov man staggered back, trying to stay out of reach. As he did, he slipped on the icy surface and went down onto a knee. His attacker then lashed out with a kick, the toe of his boot catching him in the side of the head.

Knocker winced as he saw the man's head whip back. Shatov's man fell onto his back and the Kola man dived on top, his hands locking around his opponent's throat, trying to squeeze the life from him.

In desperation, Shatov's man stabbed him in the eye with a straight finger. However, before withdrawing it from the howling man's socket, he hooked the digit and took the eyeball with it.

The fight was done from then. The Shatov man hit his distracted opponent in the throat and stunned him. The man dropped to his knees and Shatov's fighter walked around behind his opponent, picked up a chunk of rock, and smashed it into the back of the Kola man's head.

And there ended the fight. One victor, one man dead.

Knocker looked over at Kola. The man was grinding his teeth as he tried to swallow the bitter pill of defeat.

Shatov slapped Knocker on the shoulder. "And that, my friend, is how we do things in Purgatory."

"Fucking brutal," Knocker replied.

"Indeed, it is."

"What time is the truck for breakfast?" Knocker asked, feeling a shiver from the cold rippling through his body.

"We eat once a day," Shatov replied.

"What about water?" Knocker asked. "I haven't had a drink since yesterday?"

"Come."

Knocker followed him inside to a cell. It was larger than the one he was in. In the corner, there was a bucket and a tin cup. Shatov dipped it. He handed it to Knocker, who took it tentatively, peering into the cup. The Russian said, "In the winter, we melt snow for water. In the summer, we catch rain."

"What if it doesn't rain?" Knocker asked.

"Then we drink whatever we can get."

Knocker took a drink and said, "It tastes like someone pissed in it."

"Damn, Comrade. Did I dip the wrong bucket?"

Knocker stared at Shatov and the general gave a guttural laugh. "It was a joke, Englishman."

"Yeah, real funny, Comrade."

"Drink. It will not kill you."

Knocker took another sip. "Speaking of killing me. What happened to your man last night?"

"There is no need to worry about him. There will be a new man tonight. The other one is no longer in my employ."

Knocker went back to his cell and stayed there for a couple of hours. While he was lying on his cot, Kutepov came to visit him. "Do you have an answer for me?"

"Yeah, I'm not going to do it."

"It makes me disappointed to hear that."

"I'm sure you'll get over it."

"Yes, but will you?"

The guards came for Knocker that night. Which was unusual because Shatov said that they rarely stepped foot inside the prison compound. However, when they woke him, there was a reinforced squad of shooters heavily armed.

"Get up."

"What the fuck is going on?" Knocker asked.

"Come with us."

"The fuck I am."

Four men entered his cell and started to manhandle him toward the doorway. Knocker fought back, and suddenly, his head started to ring and he slouched down from the solid baton he was hit with.

Another guard stepped in behind him and hit him across the lower back, inflicting a great deal of pain. He hit him again and again until Knocker couldn't stand. Then they grabbed his arms, and as they dragged him out of the cell, he lost consciousness.

When Knocker came to, he was cold. So cold he was shivering. He was in a dark room where the blackness was absolute. He could not even see his hands in front of his face as there was no ambient light. It reminded him of a time when he'd been taken prisoner in Iraq. He and a team of SAS were working night ops, hitting HVT targets, when they rolled up on a compound supposedly holding an IED maker.

It had been a trap, and when things kicked off, three SAS operators were down, one was missing, and the remaining two were fighting for their lives against almost overwhelming numbers until help arrived.

The missing man was Knocker.

"Mr. Kane, is this going to take long?" German asked. "I do not see the relevance—"

"Do you want the whole story or just the pieces you feel like listening to?" I asked him.

"I'd rather that you didn't go off on these tangents that have no relevance to what we want to hear. Just tell us more about Shatov."

"I'm getting to that."

"Well, hurry up."

Knocker had been battered silly by a blast. When he was lucid enough to realize what was happening, he was in the hands of Iraqi insurgents.

He'd been locked away inside a pit for days. A raid by US SEALs on the new compound found him by accident when their dog sniffed him out.

Now he was back in one of those holes.

He felt the cold wall. He climbed to his feet and followed

it around until he'd done a full circuit of the cell. It was about seven feet square. Not even room to swing a cat as the saying goes.

Knocker sat back down and leaned against the cold wall. He sat there thinking about stuff, trying to keep his mind occupied. Things like old missions, old friends, trying to figure out the current mission, and going over old recipes that he knew.

Time seemed to crawl, or did it rush? He didn't know because the dark negated all sense of it.

The small trapdoor embedded in the steel door of the cell opened, letting in some light. Peering through the opening was a familiar face. "How do you like your new room?" Kutepov asked.

"I gather I have you to thank for this?"

"What can I say, I hate being told no."

"Asshole," Knocker muttered.

"You know how to get out of here, Englishman. Just say you will do what I want you to do."

Knocker gave him a mirthless grin. "Fuck off."

CHAPTER 17

It took time to get organized. Time I figured Knocker didn't have, and I was starting to get irritable by the time we were finally ready to go. Our SUV pulled up at an airfield outside of Warsaw. To avoid the FSB and all other prying eyes, we had to leave to come back. Now I was ready, but so was someone else, which came as a surprise to me at the time.

Fiona was dressed in battle kit and warm clothing. "Are you ready?"

"What are you doing?"

"I'm coming with."

"The hell you are."

She held up her MP5SD. "I didn't bring this for no reason, Mr. Kane."

I shook my head. "Shit, if you're coming with me, you'd better call me Reaper."

We got to the plane, an Ilyushin Il-76. What better plane to use? It was piloted by specially trained RAF pilots, and the aircrew took care of the rest. These men were the Royal Air Force's special forces.

"Why aren't they in the report?" Christine Ryan asked.

"They were deliberately left out," I replied. "If you understand about top secret operations, you will then understand why."

She didn't like the reply but realized it was all she was going to get. Grudgingly, she said, "Continue."

Boarding the plane, the ramp came up, grinding away. Inside was the snowcat I had requested, complete with spare fuel fixed to the outside. It was white to blend into the harsh environment.

We strapped ourselves into seats along the side of the cargo bay while the plane's turbofans sped up and started to scream. Headsets were provided so we could talk. "We were in luck, one of our assets inside the system found someone who will show us the way in."

"Can they be trusted?"

"I guess we'll find out."

The plane started moving, taxiing out to the end of the main runway. I could feel the vibrations through the airframe as it turned, and the throttles brought the turbines to fever pitch.

Then the brakes were released, and the giant bird thundered along the runway before clawing its way into the sky.

I slept most of the way and was woken by Fiona when we were close. "Five minutes, John."

I felt the Ilyushin start its descent and vibrate as the throttles came back. It bounced as turbulence got hold of it before steadying again. Fiona looked at me and said, "We're landing in a snowstorm."

"Fantastic."

The plane jerked and spasmed as it touched down. I felt it slow before one of the crew chiefs came over and said, "Time to go, sir."

Coming to my feet, I climbed into the snowcat. Fiona climbed into the passenger seat and said, "Just checking, but you have driven one of these before?"

"A couple of times."

"Oh, good."

The ramp came down and exposed the interior of the Ilyushin to the savage weather. Fiona said, "The weather is going to stay like this for the next week. It'll give us a window to get in and out and back here to the plane. It's going to remain on the ground while we're gone."

With a nod, I shoved the snowcat into reverse and gave it some gas. It lurched backward and started down the ramp. Once out into the snow, I said over the coms, "Reaper One to Falcon One-One, copy?"

"Copy, Reaper One."

The radio was crackly. "Thanks for the ride. We'll see you when we get back."

"Good luck, sir."

"You, too. Out."

The first day, we traveled north using satellite navigation. The storm never let up and I was happy for the long-range fuel tanks on the cat. Late in the afternoon, we came across an old stone hut out in the middle of nowhere. We decided to remain there until the following morning.

The hut was cold but protected against the outside weather. Someone had left some wood there a long time ago and we managed to get a fire going. That night, while we ate rations, I looked at Fiona and said, "Why did you come?"

"Couldn't leave you to go it alone," she replied. "Wouldn't be right."

"What did your boss have to say about it?"

"He wasn't happy. He told me that if I returned, he would post me back to the UK."

I nodded. "Sorry."

"No, don't be. If I knew it would happen, I would have done something like this long ago."

I chewed on some dehydrated food for a bit before asking, "This man of yours inside. Is he one of the guards?"

"Yes. He will tell us where Mr. Jensen is, and we'll need to go in to get him."

"What about the guards?"

"The guards don't go in there. Not as a rule, anyway."

I nodded. "By my thinking, we should arrive just after dark tomorrow night."

"Yes, our contact will meet us to the east of the prison."

"Then we'd better get some rest."

Meanwhile, the news of our presence in the north had reached our enemies. The Russian had received Chuzhkov in his office earlier that day. "What is it, Boris?"

"It seems you were right. They have located their friend and sent two people to get him out."

"Is Mr. Kane one of them?"

"Yes," Chuzhkov said.

"Then you'd best assemble a team to meet them."

"Already done, sir. I have twenty men ready to go just as soon as I arrive at the airfield. We should be on site by the time they arrive."

The Russian was happy with the news. "Very good. I will see you upon your return. Good luck, Boris. Do not let me down."

Chuzhkov left the office and climbed into a black SUV. He was then transported to Chkalovsky Air Base outside of Moscow. The equipment for the team was almost loaded when he arrived. He pulled his second-in-command aside. A thin-faced man who'd been with him for the past two years. His name was Danil Orlov.

"What is left to load?" Chuzhkov asked.

"Just the last vehicle."

Chuzhkov looked at the last of the articulated tracked

transports, which was going up the ramp. He nodded. "Get the men loaded, Danil. We have work to do."

Twenty minutes later, Chuzhkov was aboard the transport and seated, watching the ramp come up. Soon the turbines were screaming and the plane was taxiing. Minutes later, the heavy transport lumbered into the air with its belly full.

"This is as far as we go," I said to Fiona. "The rest we do on foot."

It was just after dark, and where I had pulled the snowcat up was about two miles from the prison. In the snowstorm, they wouldn't have seen it. Not that there was much light anyway, the daylight hours were getting shorter every day.

Readying our kit, we climbed down into the snow, donning snowshoes to make the going a little easier. The icy wind felt like the prick of fine needles upon any exposed skin. We crossed the open expanse through the darkness as we moved as best we could against the wind.

Eventually we reached the rendezvous point. It was a cave, and we found our contact inside. "Where have you been?" he asked hurriedly.

"In case you haven't noticed, it's a fucking whiteout out there," Fiona growled at him.

He grumbled something else and said, "I have to get back before I am missed."

"Where are we going?" I asked him.

"Wait," Fiona said. "Why will you be missed?"

"Some men came today and have taken over security."

My blood ran colder than it already was. "What men?"

"They are led by a man called Chuzhkov."

"Of course they are," I muttered. "Where are they?"

"Everywhere. Two of them are outside the solitary cell where your friend is located."

I looked over at Fiona. "This just got a whole lot tougher."

"We've come too far to go back now."

"I never said anything about going back," I declared. Then, looking at our contact, I asked, "How do we get to him?"

He pulled a piece of paper from his pocket. "I have drawn you a map."

Looking at it in the torchlight, I shook my head. "Where are the fucking stick figures? Did a kid draw it?"

He looked offended, but right at that time, I just didn't give a shit. "It will get you to him. The crosses are where some of the new forces are located. Here is a key that will get you through anything that is locked. Now, where is my money?"

I nodded at Fiona, who took the key. "Give it to him."

She handed over the Russian currency we'd brought for him. It equated to $1,000 US. He took it and said, "I wish you luck. You are going to need it."

He disappeared out of the cave, and I looked at the scrawled map again. "It looks like we enter here through a door. This is going to have to be as silent as possible."

"He's got guards on the door we're meant to enter through."

"Yeah, there is no getting around that. Get your comms up, put your mask on, and let's go."

We used our NVGs as we approached the prison. Gone were the snowshoes. It was fine because the snow had a good crust upon it. As we neared the door, I finally picked out the two guards. They were sheltered out of the wind, standing on a stoop.

Crawling forward until we were in range, we brought

our MP5s into line, let our laser sights settle, and I said in a low voice, "Send it."

We fired four rounds, putting the two guards down hard. "Sucks to be you."

Hurrying forward toward the door, I hid the bodies in the snow. Fiona eased the door open, and we were greeted by an open area with mesh fences set out in squares looking like separate dog pens.

All of them were open, which gave us a path through. On the other side, we were to move through a much larger room. It turned out to be a dining room. Inside were two more guards, making regular circuits to keep warm. Apart from that, they also had a large drum with a fire burning in it.

Using hand signals, I indicated for Fiona to follow me. We were hunched over, moving from table to table. The room was dull from the brown-out style lighting. I was about to move when Fiona stopped me. The second guard had changed his route and was coming our way.

We slid under the table and listened. I took my knife out and waited. I could hear his footsteps on the concrete floor, his boots crunching on the grit. We waited as they grew nearer and then held our collective breaths as his boots came into view.

He stopped. I stared hard at his feet, willing them to keep going. He turned a half circle and went back the way he'd come.

Easing out from beneath the tables, we continued slowly toward the doorway on the other side.

There was an open area of about twenty feet from the last table to the doorway. I looked to see what the guards were doing. They were both walking away. I went across first so I could cover Fiona as she crossed after me.

I reached the doorway without any trouble and then

turned to signal Fiona. "Hold," I whispered. The two guards were coming back.

She crawled under a table and waited. I ducked back around the doorway and listened to their footsteps. My finger rested on the trigger, ready to go into action if I needed to. Then the footsteps started to fade.

Looking around the doorway, I could see them walking away from our position. I waved Fiona toward me. She slid out from beneath the table and moved swiftly to my position.

"That was intense."

"Yeah," I replied.

We kept moving until reaching the main cell block. Three levels of miniature apartments built close together. I waited, watching. This was where things got tricky. We had to get through a locked door first. Once we had that open, I looked up. Each level had someone or someones on it. Noise echoed throughout the block, and it was here we had to traverse.

I guess the one bonus was that there was no one outside a cell on the bottom floor. I leaned close to Fiona. "We go around the wall. Keep close to it. If you are seen, if someone talks to you, just keep moving. If something kicks off, press forward. Do not kill anyone you don't have to. The last thing we need is a full-scale riot."

"Copy that."

"Follow me," I said to her and stepped forward.

As I moved, I all but had my shoulder against the wall, limiting the places that we were visible from. I hurried past open cell doors, trying not to attract attention. Somewhere above us, a prisoner screamed. It was a high-pitched shriek that almost chilled me to the bone. Ahead of me, a prisoner stepped out of his cell. He looked up and shouted in Russian for the prisoner to shut up.

Then he turned. Saw me. Opened his mouth to say

something, and I was forced to hit him. He dropped like a stone, out cold. I leaned down and dragged him into the cell he'd come out of. I left him on the floor and reemerged.

We kept moving and our luck held.

At the other end of the cell block, we went through the doorway. We found another large room. This one was occupied by around fifteen prisoners standing around a fire barrel. We had to get through here to reach the stairwell down to the old laundry, where we would find access to the solitary cells.

It was as though the prisoners were having a meeting. And although that was a concern, the other was the two armed men on the other side of a barred gate that separated us and them. We had to go through it. There wasn't any other way.

We eased back out of sight. "How do we do this?"

I unclipped a stun grenade. "Grab one of yours. We throw them in, which will take care of the prisoners. It will draw the guards' attention, and we take them down."

"Just like that?" Fiona asked, unhooking a stun grenade.

"That's the theory. Just don't get caught in the blast."

I nodded and we pulled the pins. We threw them toward the center of the room and ducked back.

The grenades detonated and we heard howls of pain. Fiona and I stepped into a room full of prisoners staggering around, holding onto their heads. On the other side, at the barred gate, as I predicted, the two guards had responded. We brought our MP5s up and fired before the two guards realized what was happening.

Both jerked as rounds smashed into them. They fell to the cold, hard floor and stayed down. Beside me, a prisoner starting to recover from the blast grabbed at me. I slapped his hand away and called over to Fiona, "Get the gate open."

A prisoner staggered into her, and she pushed him away. However, they were slowly gaining their senses and the first of those looked at me and started forward. My MP5 came up and pointed at his face. "Don't"

He stopped, a snarl on his face. Another prisoner joined him, then another, and soon I was facing a wall of them. All were pressing forward.

"Shit. How's that gate coming?"

"I'm having trouble with the key."

"Work the problem, Fiona."

"I'm fucking trying."

The prisoner in the center took another step forward. My aim dropped and I shot him in the meaty part of his thigh. He cried out in pain and dropped to the floor. His friends stopped, uncertainty on their faces. I knew it wouldn't hold them for long.

My back hit the wall beside the doorway barred by the gate. "Now would be good."

"It's stuck. I can't—got it."

The gate swung open, and she stepped through. I followed her and she swung it shut, locking it while I covered the prisoners. As soon as we stepped away from the gate, the prisoners rushed it like a pack of caged animals out for blood.

Now, we needed to move fast. The stairwell was next and we raced down them. At the bottom, it opened out into another large room. The old laundry still had what was left of its equipment, all of it broken or smashed up. Two large boilers, way past their use-by date, stood cold and dead.

The laundry was accessed from three areas. The way we'd come and two others. All had open doorways. I heard a cry of pain followed by the cackle of a crazed person. I eased around one of the dormant boilers and saw a prisoner crouched over a prone form. The crouching prisoner was doing something, and each time he did it, the one lying on the floor convulsed and cried out. Then I realized what it was the crouching prisoner was doing. I brought up my MP5 and shot him in the head.

"What the fuck was that?" Fiona asked.

I walked over to the man lying on the floor. Took one look and shot him too. Fiona came up beside me. She looked down and gasped. "Motherfucker."

"Wait," said Holland. "What was the reason for killing the prisoners out of hand? I can't think of any rules of engagement which condones such an act."

I stared at him. "The crazy bastard was cutting pieces off the prisoner on the floor and eating them. I did what anyone would do to a crazed animal."

"What about the prisoner on the floor? Why shoot him?"

"It had been going on for a while. You work it out."

We kept going until we reached the solitary block. Inside was another guard. I walked toward him with my weapon trained on his chest. "Drop the gun, Ivan."

He looked at me, contemplating his next move. I read his mind and said, "Don't think about it. Just do what I say, and you might live through the rest of the night."

His AK-12 clattered to the hard floor.

"Is that you, Reaper?" a familiar voice asked.

"It's me," I replied.

"About fucking time you got here. This place is a shit sandwich with all the fucking trimmings. Don't even get me started on the food."

"Open the cell, Fiona."

She used the key provided by our contact and got nowhere. "It doesn't work."

"Try the guard here."

While the Russian soldier stood still, she checked his pockets. "Got one."

Fiona tried the lock again and it turned. The door swung open, and Knocker stepped out. "Son, am I glad to see you. And you, too, Miss Fiona."

"Here." I passed him the pack I'd been carrying with all the necessaries. Weapons, ammo, body armor. Fiona had been packing warm kit.

Knocker took it and got changed. We ushered the guard into the cell and locked the door. "You ready to go?"

Knocker looked at me. "Yeah, just as soon as we get Shatov."

"Who is Shatov?" I asked, confused.

"The man who knows about The Gods of War."

I knew what he was proposing was wrong. I mean, what could go right? We were in a hellhole prison, which the prisoners more or less ran, there were special forces in the mix, and my friend drops news that we have no choice but to act upon.

"I should have left you in here," I growled at Knocker.

"Then who would keep you on your toes?"

"Where is he?"

"In the main cell block."

"He would be. All right, let's go and get him. And God help us all."

CHAPTER 18

Chuzhkov loaded his AK-12 and looked at Danil. "Deploy the rest of the men. He is in here somewhere."

The Russian had set up his command post in the former security room, which had once been the heartbeat of the penal camp. Danil nodded. "Like I said, I've lost contact with five of them. They are already searching. The problem is that the prisoners not being locked up makes it harder. There are some places that our men should not go. The best way is to wait. Hit them when they come out. Set up a perimeter to watch. Going in there will just get more of our men killed. With a little luck, the prisoners might do our job for us."

The special forces leader nodded. "All right, Danil, we'll do it your way. Wake the prisoners up. Let's see what happens."

"We have to go back through there," I said, looking at the locked gate with the still-angry prisoners on the other side. "I don't know of a way—"

An old air raid siren shattered the night. Knocker spat on the floor. "That fucked that, Reaper."

"You ready to go to work?"

"Don't you Yanks say I was born ready?"

"Shit." I looked at Fiona. "Do not hesitate. It will get you killed."

"Roger that," she replied nervously.

I stared at her. "Hey, it's OK to be scared, it'll keep you alive. Now, open that gate."

She nodded and went to the gate. She was there all of ten seconds before she was seen. It took ten more to open it. Then I stepped through into the bowels of hell.

I didn't want to just kill everyone in front of me, so I aimed low, taking the legs. Three prisoners went down while their friends pressed forward. I drew my handgun and used it as a club, battering my way forward.

With MP5 in one hand and Glock in the other, I made inroads into a growing throng. Beside me, Knocker wasn't as forgiving as I was. He shot a knife-wielding prisoner in the chest with a three-round burst before putting a bullet between the eyes of another. He called back over his shoulder, "Fiona, watch our six."

It was then that I realized that they were closing in behind us. The raging battle reminded me of a zombie movie where the walking dead were closing in on their prey.

I heard Fiona open fire through the din but didn't look to see what she was doing. I had my own hands full. Smashing a prisoner in the face with the MP5, I then shot one beside him in the chest with my handgun. This one fell into a heap at my feet.

Suddenly he was replaced by a snarling figure wielding a homemade machete. The time was well and truly gone to be choosy. I shot him in the head and moved on.

Beside me, Knocker growled as a knife opened a cut in his left arm. "Dirty rotten fucker. See if you like this."

He shot his attacker three times. Then, after the man fell, he shot him again. Behind us, Fiona was still holding her own, keeping the prisoners off our backs.

After a short while, they started to fall back, giving us more room. We pressed on toward the doorway. Once we reached it, we moved into the main cell block.

It was like walking out of hell and into Armageddon. I dropped out the magazine from the MP5 and the other from the handgun, reloading both. Prisoners were everywhere, and among it all, somewhere was the man we needed to find.

"Up this way," Knocker said as he started climbing a set of steel stairs. A prisoner appeared on the landing above and started down. However, instead of doing anything toward us, he pushed past and joined the throng below. We climbed higher, and when we reached the landing, Knocker proceeded along it. Another prisoner appeared in front of him. Eyes wild, a knife in his hand. He lunged at Knocker and missed. Knocker pushed his handgun forward and let off four shots, each hammering into his attacker and making him jerk. Then he tipped the corpse over the rail so that it crashed onto the crowd below.

Another prisoner appeared in front of him, and Knocker hit him between the eyes with his handgun. The man dropped like a stone to the gantry.

Knocker kept on until he reached the cell he wanted. He turned to go inside and uttered a curse. I followed him in, and he was already crouched over a fallen man. He looked up at me, "He's been stabbed, Reaper."

I crouched down while Fiona secured the entrance to the cell. The man at our feet was still alive, but only just. He looked up at Knocker and grinned faintly. "I am dead, my English friend."

He coughed, and his chest rattled as his lungs were filling with blood. "Who did this, General?"

"Kutepov."

"Damn it. I need to know about The Gods of War, General."

He nodded vaguely. "You can't—can't let them do it."

"Do what?"

"The president is being impeached," I said hurriedly.

"Then—then it has started."

"What has started?" I asked.

"I was one of them you—you know. Until they started talking about it," Shatov said, talking in riddles.

"About what?"

His mouth opened and closed, but nothing came out.

"Come on, Mikhail, hang in there," Knocker said.

"They—they need to replace the—the president to…" his voice trailed away.

I felt for a pulse and found nothing. He was gone. And with it, what he knew about the plan.

"Fuck," I hissed.

"We need to go, lads," Fiona said. "I'm starting to draw some attention. I think it might be the fact that I have tits."

We climbed to our feet, leaving Shatov where he lay.

Knocker said, "Kutepov wanted me to kill him. Said he could get me out of here. That man there was tough but fair. That's probably why they didn't like him."

Fiona fired her MP5. "Move, damn it. You can cry later."

We went back out onto the gantry and made for the far end, where the stairs would bring us down to where we wanted to be.

A big hulk of a man stepped in front of me as I started down. He roared like a bear and flexed his muscles. No shit, this guy was huge. So I did the first thing that came into my mind. I shot him, right? No, I kicked him under the chin.

His head jerked up, his eyes rolled back in his head, and he fell like a tree.

Glass jaw.

When I reached the ground floor, a crowd of prisoners ran in our direction. I opened fire at their legs and brought down the first few, making the others stop where they were. We ducked through the doorway that would eventually lead us into the dining hall. I looked left and saw a gate made of steel bars. I grabbed it and started to close it on the surging crowd.

It screeched in protest, but I had it shut when they reached it. "Fiona, lock it."

She tried the key, but nothing happened. Meanwhile, I was leaning all my weight against the gate.

"I can't get it to lock," Fiona said.

One of the prisoners hit the fingers of my left hand with something and I dragged it back. "Christ. Knocker, grab my last flashbang."

He grabbed it and pulled the pin, throwing it into the cell block. I put my head down and covered my ears as best I could. Then it detonated. Every man inside the cell block scattered, and while they panicked, we ran.

The dining hall was empty, which made our passage through it a lot quicker than the first time. However, when we got to the yard, things were different. The dog pens, as I knew them, were still empty, but there were soldiers on the walls. Things were about to get a whole lot more interesting.

I ducked back. Knocker came up to my shoulder. "What's up?"

"We've got shooters on the walls. They have to be Chuzhkov's men."

"What do you want to do?" Knocker asked.

I said, "Shoot and scoot. I'll go first, then you, then

Fiona. We leapfrog each other as we go, laying down cover fire."

Knocker nodded. "See you in hell."

I grinned at him. "We're already there." I looked at Fiona. "You'll be fine."

With my MP5 up, ready to fire, I broke cover. Behind me, Knocker started firing at the first figure on the wall. This was the easy part. This guy dropped dead, but now his buddies were alerted to what was happening. So, they opened fire.

Near a post that held up the fencing, I stopped so I could get a clear shot. As soon as I opened fire, Knocker ran toward me while Fiona took up his position and began firing.

When he reached me, he took up a firing position, and we covered Fiona as she came our way. We kept leapfrogging each other, suppressing the shooters on the wall. At one point I heard Knocker grunt and he staggered. "Are you all right?"

"Caught a round in a plate."

By the time we reached the gate, we'd brought down two more shooters. I opened it and immediately received incoming fire from shooters hiding behind a truck that hadn't been there on the way in. I pulled two fragmentation grenades and gave Knocker one. "Throw and go."

"Roger that."

I turned to Fiona. "As soon as the frags blow, we run. Do not stop."

Knocker and I pulled the pins and threw the grenades. When they detonated, the truck blew up and the blast cast a bright orange hue across the snow. But we weren't there for pretty sights.

We ran. All three of us, heads down, asses up, running for our lives. Bullets chasing us as we went. Once we were clear of the light, we were safer. Not home, but safer.

Shouts and gunfire continued behind us, bullets cracking as they passed us too close for comfort. Then the shooting stopped, replaced by the roar of vehicles. Headlights appeared, scything left and right as they tried to find us. All we had to do was remain one step ahead of them until we reached the snowcat. Then, and only then, would we have an even chance.

"Fiona, you drive," I said as we climbed into the snowcat. We were all blowing hard, and in the distance through the snowstorm, we could hear the vehicles but not see their lights. So far, we had been lucky.

Fiona started the cat and engaged it into gear. It lurched forward and she got it going in the right direction. I looked over my shoulder at Knocker, who was sitting back with his eyes closed. "Are you OK?"

"Fine. Wake me if shit happens."

"No problem."

We drove through what remained of the rest of the night before stopping at the stone hut we'd used on the way in.

"I'll take first watch," Knocker said.

"No, I'll do it," I replied. "Get some rest."

He and Fiona rested fitfully while we waited. That's what it was all about, waiting for the Russian special forces. We were better with solid cover than getting caught out in the open.

They found us two hours later.

"Knocker, wake up," I said, gently shaking him. "They're here."

"What's the weather like, Reaper?"

"Good for us," I replied.

I went over to the inside wood pile and started moving some of the logs. Before long, I had enough of them clear, leaning down and pulling up some floorboards. I reached down into the void beneath and retrieved a long object wrapped in cloth. Unwinding the cover revealed a Dragunov sniper rifle.

"Is that for me?" Knocker asked.

"If you want it."

He took it and headed toward the door. "Don't start without me."

"Where is he going?" Fiona asked.

"To have some fun."

The headlights came out of the storm like four golden orbs. They stopped and I saw the figures emerge from both articulated tracked vehicles. In my ear, I heard Knocker say, "On your word, Reaper. In position."

"Send it."

As I watched, I saw a figure fall. The sound of the storm blocked out the noise of the suppressed Dragunov. Before they realized what was happening, a second soldier had fallen.

Then Knocker said, "Shifting position."

Fiona and I watched the soldiers scatter in the storm. Out there somewhere was Chuzhkov and I owed him blood. I walked toward the door. Fiona called after me. "Where are you going?"

"To see an old friend."

The storm had eased but not much. Snow still fell in a thin curtain. I said into my comms, "Knocker, I'm out. Don't shoot me."

"Then don't step in front of a bullet," he replied.

I circled around to the right, ready to fire if and when I needed to. And I needed to. A soldier appeared in front of me, and the first thing I did was hesitate. It was stupid, a man of my training hesitating. If it had been under different circumstances, I possibly would have been killed. But the only explanation that came to me was that he thought I was one of his comrades. When I squeezed the trigger, he found out otherwise.

A burst of fire from the MP5 punched into his chest armor. He staggered back but was still alive. I fired again. This time, the rounds ripped through his throat, and one hammered into his skull.

"Nice, Reaper. A little slow, but nice," Knocker said.

I heard a bullet crack past my head and a grunt came from my left. My head snapped around and I saw another soldier falling to the snow.

Up until this point, Knocker had killed two more. We were thinning their numbers slowly, but we were still outnumbered. I kept circling, closing on their vehicles as I went. Bullets from their weapons reached out through the storm, trying to find a target. I could see the outline of another figure close to a vehicle. I brought my MP5 up and fired.

A cry of pain told me he was still alive, but when he'd fallen, he'd disappeared. A storm of bullets came my way and I dived into the snow. I could hear the rounds hitting all around me.

Meanwhile, Knocker was still in the fight. He'd shifted position again and fired two more shots at another target.

By now, the soldiers were thinned out quite a bit. From the ones we'd killed at the prison and those here at the hut, Chuzhkov was down a few men. Not that we knew he was still alive at the time. For all we knew, we could have got lucky and killed him in the snow.

"I've got two shooters coming at me from the west," Fiona said.

"Can you handle it?"

"I think so."

"Knocker?"

"I see them."

While they took care of that threat, I moved closer to the

articulated tracked vehicles. If Chuzhkov was anywhere, this would be it. He'd been losing men at a steady rate, and now he'd be backed into a corner. The most dangerous animal of all.

I crept around the tracked vehicles, looking for any more special forces soldiers. As I emerged from the rear of one, bullets peppered the armored skin as someone opened fire at me. I ducked back as more bullets ricocheted off the vehicle into the snow-filled night. I pulled back and circled around the other way. "Knocker, can you see him?"

"No such luck, Reaper. I can't get a line on him."

More bullets peppered the other end of the tracked articulate. I emerged from cover and fired toward where the shots were originating. The incoming fire stopped as the shooter was forced into cover.

Reloading, I took a punt. I exposed myself from where I was hiding and opened fire. With each burst I was walking forward. The suppressive fire had the desired effect. No more incoming.

What I didn't know was that Chuzhkov had outsmarted me. He'd changed position, and I found out about the same time he hit me from the side will all the force he could muster in his body.

Both of us crashed down into the snow, rolling around. He was trying to get the upper hand, I was trying to get my breath. When he'd struck, he'd driven all the air from my lungs.

I managed to get the growling special forces boss off me. He rolled away and came up onto his knees. His hand went for the Grach he had in a thigh holster. I reached for my own weapon, but it wasn't there. Throwing myself forward, I grabbed at his wrist so he couldn't bring his weapon up.

His snarl grew into a roar. "Why don't you just fucking die?"

"Why don't you?" I asked and hit him with a closed fist.

Once.

Twice.

Then he heaved his body upward and I rolled off and away.

Chuzhkov came to his feet, and I did the same. He dipped his shoulder and charged, hitting me in my middle, and I could feel his strength course through his body. I went backward and slammed against one of their armored vehicles. I let out a muffled cry of pain and brought down a fist onto his back to try and break his hold. Nothing happened, and I was forced to do it three more times.

Chuzhkov released me and staggered back. I stepped in close and hit him twice more, both blows rocking him back onto his heels. He had a lot of blood flowing but was far from done. You don't live this long in war zones by giving up. Reaching to his hip, his hand came up with a knife.

The Russian lunged at me, waving the blade like a sword. I stepped aside and then back as it caught my cold-weather clothing. I heard the fabric tear and felt a thin, burning sensation on my arm. He'd got me, and he knew it.

"Did the little knife bite you, Kane?" he growled.

"I'm still in the fight, Chuzhkov. First you, and then your master."

"You won't stop them," he gloated. "It is too late. The wheels have already begun to turn."

He lunged at me again and I took another step back. My foot found a rock under the snow, causing me to lose my balance. My arms windmilling, I fell backward. Now I was vulnerable with Chuzhkov standing over me.

"Now I have—"

WHAP!

His head snapped to the side, and he dropped like a stone. In my ear over the comms, I heard Knocker say, "Eat shit, motherfucker."

I lay there for a moment, gasping, sucking in deep breaths. Then I said, "Is that all of them?"

"You're welcome," came the reply.

"Fiona, are you all right?"

"Remind me never to go anywhere with you guys again."

I climbed to my feet and shook my head, wiping snow from my arms and back. "Come on, we've got a plane to catch."

CHAPTER 19

We flew back to Moscow via Warsaw into a storm. When we reached the embassy, we were debriefed by Kruger. "You lot have blown up a shit storm once again, but that is the least of our problems. The Duma went all the way with their impeachment and forced their president out. It took a matter of hours. Both us and the Americans are trying to get an audience with the new president, but there's nothing forthcoming."

"Who is the new president?" Fiona asked.

"Sergey Lash."

"Who is Sergey Lash?" I asked.

"His father was hardline KGB back in the eighties," Kruger said. "Said to have killed more defectors in East Germany than anyone on record. He got his father's ideologies and went into politics when he was old enough. He picked up a following along the way. If he gets his way, the iron curtain will come back up overnight, and all the former USSR states will come back under his control."

"When Shatov was dying, he said we couldn't let them succeed," Knocker said.

"Who is Shatov?" Kruger asked.

"He claims he was once one of The Gods of War. He was a Russian general."

"I'll look into him."

I said, "When Chuzhkov thought he had me, he said that we were too late, things had already started."

"I guess he means the impeachment," Kruger said. "So, what now?"

"We go after the Russian," I said. "If we can find him."

Kruger's cell rang. He stepped away and took the call. After speaking for a few minutes, he returned to us. "That went to shit, fast."

"What's up?"

"The new president's first order of the day has been to order us and the Americans out of the country. We have three days to get everything in order and then we're gone."

"Bollocks. That was quick," Knocker said.

"So we have three days to find our Russian friend," I mused, stroking my chin thoughtfully.

"How the fuck are we meant to do that, Reaper, when we don't even know his name?"

Kruger nodded in agreement. "You are on the clock."

"We dig into Shatov."

Fiona nodded. "Then it's about time we got started."

We went to work trying to find out what we could about Shatov. He had been a career soldier who had served in the Afghanistan war in the eighties. Eventually, he was promoted to general and there was nothing else.

"Was he married?" Knocker asked.

Fiona hit a few keys on the computer. "Yes, but his wife died two years ago."

"Bastard."

"He did have a son, though."

I looked at Knocker. "Might be worth a look."

He nodded. "Where does he live?"

"Here in Moscow."

"Then let's go and see him. We'll need an address and name."

Fiona said, "Denis Shatov. I'll send you the address. Meanwhile, I'll stay here and see if I can come up with something on our other friend."

Fortunately, Shatov's son didn't live too far from the embassy. A two-floor, narrow-looking home on a quiet street with a streetlamp out front and a paved sidewalk.

It was dark outside except for the orange streetlamp. Inside the house, lights were on, which indicated that somebody might be home. I knocked on the door and waited. When the door opened, we were greeted by a thin man with a tired-looking face and graying hair. He gave us a confused look. "Who are you?"

"My name is John, this is Raymond."

"Yes."

"We're here to ask you about your father."

"You are American?"

"Yes."

"My father is dead for years." He started to close the door until I stopped him.

"No, he died a couple of days ago."

He frowned. "You are mistaken."

"I saw him die. Please let us in and we will explain everything."

He hesitated and then stepped back. "Please, come in."

Shatov's son showed us through to a sitting room and invited us to sit on a sofa. "Would you like coffee?"

I shook my head. "No, thank you. We won't keep you long."

He waited for me to continue. "You said your father had been dead for years. How many?"

"Ever since I was a boy. But you said he died a couple of days ago. How can this be?"

"He's been locked away in a penal prison named Purgatory. Above the Arctic Circle."

"But how do you know this?"

I told him a little and Knocker filled him in on the rest. We gave him a little time to digest the information before Knocker asked, "What do you know about your father's military career?"

"Not a lot. I know he served in Afghanistan, and then when he returned home, he was promoted to general. It wasn't long after that we were told he was killed in a plane crash."

"Did he do any secret work that you know of?"

"If he did, he didn't say. Why do you want to know? Are you spies?"

"No, we're not spies. But something is happening and we're trying to find out what it is."

"What do you mean?"

I told him about the massacre in Syria, leaving out some of the bits I didn't think he needed to know. "Did your father have any close friends he used to spend time with before you were told he died?"

"I can only ever remember one friend that he had. Pavel."

"Who is Pavel?" I asked.

"Pavel Krupin. He was another soldier too."

"Was he a general?"

Denis nodded. "Yes."

"Do you know where we might find him?" Knocker asked.

"He's dead. He died on the same plane my father was said to have died on."

I looked at Knocker. I could see in his eyes he was wondering the same thing I was. If the Russian was Krupin.

"I have a picture of them together," Denis said.

"Do you mind if we see it?"

"Sure."

He left the room and returned moments later, passing me an old photo in a wooden frame. There were two men in it, both in uniform. A young boy was standing between them, his father's arm around him. They were outside somewhere, standing under a tree. "Who took the photo?"

"My mother."

One thing was settled at least. Neither one of them was the Russian. I said, "Your father looks happy. He has a big smile."

Denis chuckled. "No, that's Pavel. My father is the man who isn't smiling."

"Sorry, I thought the man with his arm around you was your father."

I looked over at Knocker. It was a sharp glance. A questioning glance. But we'd both come to the same conclusion. The man who had died in Purgatory. The man we knew as Mikhail Shatov, was actually Pavel Krupin. So what the hell had happened to Mikhail Shatov?

Denis took the photo back, glancing at it sadly before reaching out to place it on the mantel above the fireplace. He took two steps before I heard the sharp sound of breaking glass, followed by a grunt. Denis turned and looked at me, his eyes wide in shock. For a moment, I wondered what had happened then I saw the spreading stain on his white shirt. He'd been shot.

I started forward off the sofa and made it halfway before the second shot came. The bullet punched a hole in Shatov's head, finishing what the first round had started. Denis fell dead on the floor, his blood soaking the cream-colored mat he'd landed on. Beside him was the photo of the two men.

"Sniper!" Knocker exclaimed as he came off the sofa onto the floor.

I smashed the glass in the frame and grabbed the photo, stuffing it inside my coat while Knocker rolled onto his back, drew his Grach handgun, and fired twice, blowing the light bulb apart and darkening the room.

Another round came in and slammed into the floor near us. We began crawling toward the doorway to get out of the room. Suddenly the front door flew open and three armed men rushed in.

Knocker fired from the hallway floor where he'd crawled to. Coming up onto a knee, I opened fire with the handgun I'd managed to get out by this time.

Single rounds were joined by the staccato sound of automatic gunfire. Fortunately, the shooters had aimed too high and made a new hole pattern in the wallpaper on either side of the hallway.

I dragged Knocker to his feet while continuing to fire. I shoved him along the hallway and shouted, "Move! Move!"

As I blew through the rest of the magazine in the handgun, I saw a shooter go down. By this time, we were in the kitchen. Knocker ran toward a large sliding glass door. Without bothering to try and open it, he fired his weapon at the glass and ran right through.

The glass fell upon us like razor-shards of confetti. Bullets chased us outside, and in front of me, Knocker jinked left and headed down along the narrow path that ran up the side of the home. I threw a look over my shoulder but saw nothing.

Emerging back at the front of the house, we came under fire from the sniper. "Fucking bollocks," I heard Knocker call out. "I forgot about that bastard."

Another round came in and a pot plant leaped as the bullet struck. We reached our vehicle and got in. The SUV was armored, but it never fails to give chills when you hear them hammer into the exterior.

Knocker started the vehicle and floored the gas pedal. It did a U-turn in the street, and as he straightened, two shooters appeared in front of us, their weapons speaking volumes.

"Run them down!" I called out to him.

He changed direction marginally and pointed the front of the SUV straight at them.

At the last moment, they leaped aside and we roared past.

"Christ, Reaper, these guys just don't fucking give up."

"Yeah, they're—Look out!"

From a side street roared a Tigr Infantry Mobility Vehicle. Knocker swerved as it tried to barrel into the side of us but missed. Its driver swung hard on the wheel and brought it skidding around.

Looking in the rearview mirror, Knocker said, "Bad news, Reaper. That thing has a weapons system on it."

"What kind?"

Just then, it fired, and an explosion rocked our SUV. "Bollocks. The kind that goes boom."

I glanced in the side mirror and saw that it had been joined by two more sets of headlights. "We've got more company back there."

The automated weapon on the Tigr fired twice more. Both missed, but not by much. I felt the concussive force batter the SUV. I glanced at Knocker. "Are you going to drive faster or let them just blow the shit out of us?"

He got grumpy. "Have you ever noticed that whenever we're running away from assholes in a fucking car that I'm always the one driving? Huh? You know what—"

BOOM!

"I finally figured it out. It's because when we die, you'll have someone else to blame."

He swung hard on the wheel and the SUV skidded to the right. He straightened it up and floored the gas once more.

I looked out the back and saw the vehicles make the turn. Orange lights flickered off their windscreens as they pursued us. I reached for my cell and called Fiona. "Listen up. We're coming in hot to the embassy with bad guys on our tail. Shatov's son is dead. They killed him."

"Good lord. I'll tell the gate to be expecting you."

"You do that. We're about three miles out."

I disconnected the call and said, "They're expecting us."

Knocker made another turn and put us on track to reach the embassy. As we went flat out along the street, everything flashed past. Bullets peppered the rear of the SUV, and an explosion made a Lada rear up like a bucking bronco.

"We're almost there," Knocker called across to me. "Just ahead."

Suddenly it felt as though we were weightless as the rear of the SUV lifted up. The back window disintegrated, showering us with glass. Hot flames ignited by the blast licked at us and then withdrew. The back of the SUV lifted even further and went past the perpendicular before crashing down onto its roof.

By some miracle, we were both conscious and only suffered a few cuts and abrasions. I released my seatbelt and landed on the roof. Knocker did the same. "Fucking hell."

"What was that?" I asked him as I crawled out of the passenger window.

"See, I fucking told you," he snarled at me. "You just want someone else to blame."

I looked around. We were upside down outside the embassy gates. Gunfire erupted and we were forced to take cover.

I took out my side arm and started shooting back at the killers who'd just arrived behind the Tigr. I went through what was left of the magazine in no time then dropped out the empty and reloaded. Beside me, Knocker was firing furiously as well. Gone was the fire discipline we'd used so many times.

The Tigr fired and we hit the asphalt, our arms over our

heads. The blast hit the other side of the SUV and moved it a couple of feet in our direction. I could hear shouting and I looked back. The gates to the embassy were open and the Marines on guard there were waving at us to run.

I looked at Knocker, who was firing again. "Hey, follow me."

"Where we going?"

"About ninety feet."

"Lead on."

I took a couple of deep breaths and started running, my mind screaming, *bullet magnet*. Rounds snapped close and kicked up asphalt around my feet. Behind me, I could hear Knocker running as fast as me. Another blast buffeted us, but once again, we were lucky.

Then we were safe. We doubled over, sucking in deep breaths. I felt the sudden urge to vomit and hurled what contents I had inside my stomach up onto the concrete drive. The firing had stopped, and I walked over to the gates and peered through.

He was there, standing across the other side of the street, flanked by two armed men. He held up a cell and dialed. My own cell buzzed.

I hit answer, and a voice said, "You seem to have an uncanny ability of escaping me, Mr. Kane."

"Who are you?" I asked him. "What is your name?"

"Names are just labels," the Russian replied. "What I wanted to do was ask you to stop interfering in our plans. After all, they have nothing to do with you."

"You made it my business when you massacred a whole village for oil," I shot back at him.

I heard him sigh. "You cannot beat us, Mr. Kane. It is too late for that. Everything is starting to be put into motion."

"By us, you mean you and your fellow Gods?"

He paused.

"Nothing to say? Cat got your tongue?"

"Stay out of our way, Mr. Kane. This is bigger than you."

The line went dead, and I watched as he walked away into the darkness. Knocker walked over. "That our friend?"

I nodded.

"What did he want?"

"Told me to give up."

Knocker chuckled. "You just know that isn't going to happen."

"Yeah, but he doesn't. Come on, let's go and talk to Fiona."

We went inside and had our cuts and grazes seen to. Then we found the MI6 contingent already packing and shredding. Fiona was discussing something with Kruger. They turned and looked at us. Kruger said, "You two certainly know how to make an entrance."

"Not our fault."

"What happened?" Fiona asked.

"They killed Denis Shatov." I reached inside my coat and took out the picture. I handed it to Fiona.

"What am I looking at?"

"The kid is Denis Shatov. The happy guy is who we thought was Mikhail Shatov."

"The prisoner who died?" Fiona asked.

"That's right. Except it isn't. That is Pavel Krupin. He was a friend of Shatov. Both men were generals in the Russian army. Both were meant to have died in a plane crash—the same plane crash—years ago."

Kruger looked at me and then at Knocker. "But why would Krupin be in a prison in Northern Russia posing as Shatov?"

"More to the point," I replied. "Where is Shatov?"

"Do you think he's mixed up in this?" Kruger asked.

"He could be. The other question is, how many of them are there, and what is their ultimate goal?"

Fiona had gone quiet. When I looked, she appeared deep

in concentration over her secure tablet. She looked up. "Krupin had a wife and two children."

I looked at Kruger. "There is your leverage."

"Which was possibly why he wanted out," Knocker said.

"Where are they?" I asked.

"Belarus."

Kruger said, "Do you want to question them?"

Shaking my head, I said, "No. They won't know much. Besides, us going there will only put a big target on their backs."

"So what now?" Fiona asked.

"Back to London and regroup," I said. "Piece together what we have and try to make sense of it."

"I'll organize a flight for you."

Kruger shook our hands. "I can't say I won't be sorry to see the back of you. You two attract trouble like flies to dog shit."

"It's a thing we have," I replied with a grin.

"Get out of here. Fiona will look after you."

CHAPTER 20

We were taken from Heathrow to a secret location where we were met by Holly Smith and Brian Short. When we got inside, they ushered us into a room and we all sat down. Short started the conversation with a short sentence. "You boys fucked up."

"How do you figure that?" I asked. "Think about it."

"If anything, we uncovered something way bigger than anything you've ever dealt with before."

"Like what?"

"I don't know, everything is still fluid."

He gave a derisive snort and I felt like busting him in the mouth. "All right, let's go through what we know."

I nodded. "The villagers were killed because of oil. Sarah Nash was killed because she was there and because she saw something she wasn't meant to."

"Right, we know that," Holly said.

"That was why they came after us. Because we stumbled across what they were doing."

"Uh, huh."

"They also were killing—we assume they were—members of the Duma to be able to have the numbers to impeach their president and get him out. Then they replaced him with a hardliner."

"But, why?" Holly asked.

"I guess it has something to do with what they're doing," Knocker said. "And the first thing he did was expel the British and the Americans."

"Also, Germany, France, Australia, and Canada."

This surprised me. I hadn't heard it since being on the plane. "All western powers," I said.

"Yes."

"It looks like he's starting a new Cold War," Knocker said.

"It would seem so. What else do you have?"

"When Knocker was in prison, he met a former general named Shatov. Mikhail Shatov. Except it wasn't him, it was another former general named Pavel Krupin. It looks like he'd been forced to take on Shatov's identity."

"Why?" Holly asked.

"Here is where things get even more interesting. He said he was locked up around five years ago when he wanted out."

"Wanted out?"

"He wanted nothing more to do with what they were doing?"

"Who?"

"The Gods of War."

"There's that whole Gods of War thing again," Short said.

"They're out there," I said. "And they're up to something big. The Russian is part of it. We still don't know who he is. His right hand, Chuzhkov, we managed to kill when we busted Knocker out of prison. You should assume Shatov is part of it, and God knows how many more."

"Yes, but what is their ultimate goal?"

"I have no idea."

"Then what do you propose we do?"

"Keep working the problem," I said. "Something will turn up."

"Are you saying that you want to stay on with MI6, Mr. Kane?"

"At least until we can sort this thing out," I replied.

"What about you, Mr. Jensen?" Short asked.

"We come as a team, me and Reaper. I watch his back and he lets me."

Short sighed. "All right, I'll assign Holly to be your handler. But if this thing goes nowhere, then you're out of here."

Short left us and Holly said, "Do you chaps have any idea what you've just done?"

I shook my head. "I'm guessing we'll find out."

"Well, where to?"

"I have a contact in Europe I might be able to reach out to. He might know something."

"Fine, try that." She stared at us. "Do not make me regret this."

TWO WEEKS LATER—HELSINKI, FINLAND

I got off the tram and started walking along the street. The night air was cool and the pavement damp where the rain had fallen earlier in the afternoon. I had arrived in Helsinki early that morning after receiving a message from my contact.

Armo was a member of the Finnish Security and Intelligence Service. I knew him from back in my days at Global. I'd also had dealings with him when working for Interpol.

My boots made a grinding sound against the damp grit of the sidewalk with every step I made. When I was about halfway along the street, I crossed over and took a narrow alley paved with cobblestones.

Walking toward me, a couple were arm in arm, the woman with her head on the man's shoulder. I heard her giggle as they went past, it was a fruity kind of laughter.

When I emerged from the alley, I turned left on another street. There were a few more pedestrians on this one, some stopping to look in storefront windows as they made their way along.

I watched as a dark BMW drove past, making sure that it was on the level and not a danger to my presence. Further along was a small café. One which opened in the evenings. I stopped at one of the outdoor tables and took a seat. A young woman wearing black pants, a T-shirt, and an apron came out and greeted me, taking my order and then clearing a table beside me of the cups left by the previous patrons.

Minutes later, she returned with a coffee and a complimentary biscuit. Then I waited.

"Hello, old friend." I looked up and saw Armo's lined face smiling at me. "It is good to see you again."

I took the hand he offered. "And you too, Armo. Please, sit." I gestured to the seat opposite me.

He sat and ordered a coffee. When it arrived he sipped it and said, "I was surprised to hear from you, John. I thought you were getting out."

"There is always someone on the other end pulling me back in," I replied. My eyes glanced at a couple as they walked past.

"I see you are cautious. It is good that you are." He held up a folder and said, "These people are not ones to mess around with."

"Who are they, Armo?" I asked.

He gave me the file. "A present. From me to you."

I opened it and saw only sheets of paper. The absence of any photos was concerning.

Armo said, "They are called The Gods of War."

"Yeah, we found that out."

I ran through some of what we knew. When I got to the subject of the Russian and Shatov, Armo said, "They are very dangerous, no one has any photos of them."

I took out the one that I had acquired at Denis Shatov's home. I pointed at the general and said, "Shatov. No one has seen him for years."

"And you say he's still alive?"

"There is a good possibility. His friend was posing as him in a hellhole above the Arctic Circle."

I looked back down at the file. Armo said, "They have been around since the sixties. A secret cadre within the KGB. They were responsible for a lot of things, but even then, they were so secretive we never had pictures."

"How many?"

"No one knows."

"Are there any whispers about what they're up to?"

Armo took a sip of coffee. "Nothing. But it must be big."

I closed the file. "Thanks for your help, Armo."

"I am just sorry I could not be of more assistance, John," he replied.

I finished my coffee and stood up, taking his hand in mine. "Goodbye."

"Be careful, old friend, these are very dangerous times."

I turned to walk away when I heard the subsonic bullet hit my friend. He grunted and doubled over. "Armo!"

He crashed onto the damp pavement, and I rushed to his side. Another bullet came from the darkness. This one was meant for me but had missed. I ducked behind the table and looked up over it. I saw a figure in the dark shadows across the street in an alley mouth. Taking out my Glock, I opened fire. My shots missed, but they had the desired effect. The shooter pulled back out of sight.

I ran across the street to the alley, my weapon raised just in case the shooter appeared. I looked around the corner and saw whoever it was running out the other end.

Continuing along the alley until I reached the end, I looked in the direction the shooter had taken. I stopped. Whoever it was had disappeared. "Shit."

Turning, I hurried back to where Armo lay. The waitress was bent over him trying to stop the bleeding. I crouched down and grabbed his hand. I could see that he was fading fast. "I'm sorry, Armo. I'm sorry I dragged you into this."

"It—it is all right, my friend. You must stop them."

"I promise, Armo. I promise."

Then he died, eyes open, looking up at the cloudy sky overhead.

A couple of days later, The Gods of War were planning their next move. They sat at a rectangular table in a hidden location in Moscow. All wore uniforms of the former USSR. It resembled some kind of SMERSH meeting from the old Bond movies.

The man at the head of the table said, "Where are we at with the British Intelligence people?"

"We have been trying to stay one step ahead of them," the Russian said. "As it turns out, they are quite capable."

"Why aren't they dead?"

"They have the lives of a cat—of many cats."

"Whatever. They cannot stop us now that things are progressing," the head of the table said. "What about the new oil field?"

"Ahead of schedule. We should start shipping in a few days."

"Good. I will inspect it in a couple of days."

"Are you sure that is wise?" the Russian asked.

"It will be fine. Now, what about our new president?"

"Reacting to each string we pull," another officer said. "By the time we are ready, he will be too. He was a great choice."

The officer at the head of the table nodded. "What about the next part of the operation?"

"I will be taking care of that," a different officer said. "Our friends are expecting another shipment of weapons soon, and I want to be there to ensure the transaction goes smoothly. Especially with our advisers on the ground."

"Keep a low profile. Try not to draw any attention to yourself."

"Yes. You can count on me."

The man at the head of the table nodded. "I guess that will do for now. Everyone may leave."

All the other generals got up and left bar one. The man we knew as The Russian stayed back. His commander looked at him and asked, "Was there something else?"

"I just wanted to say how sorry I was about your son, Mikhail."

Shatov stared at the man in front of him and said, "It was unavoidable. Besides, he stopped being my son when I chose this life over my former one."

The Russian nodded.

"Was there anything else?"

"No, sir."

"Then what about joining me when I go to Syria?"

"It would be an honor."

"So be it."

Three days later, Knocker and I were called in to see Holly Smith. She was seated at a desk with a piece of paper face down in front of her. Looking up as we entered, she said, "Gentlemen, it's good to see you. Please, take a seat."

Her hair was trimmed shorter than it was the first time we'd met her. "I gather you have some news?" I asked.

She nodded. "I do. Yesterday, we received intelligence from Syria. They have started shipping oil from the new field. It looks like the Russians are using a shell company to work it through. We tried to track it, but it was impossible. However—"

She picked up the piece of paper and slid it across the desk. It was a photo. I picked it up and passed it over to Knocker after having a look at it. When he was finished, he put it back on the desk. Face up.

I glanced at it again. Two men. The first was The Russian. I'd have known him anywhere. The second, even though the picture was grainy, was Mikhail Shatov.

"I guess that puts to rest the story about him being dead," I said.

"You sending us after him?" Knocker asked.

Holly shook her head. "No. It would be a waste of time. This was only part of the reason I wanted you in here. I have another job for you."

"Where to this time?" Knocker asked.

"You are off to Karachi. An arms shipment. I will be coming with you along with some support staff. You have two hours to get your stuff organized and be back here."

I stared at her. "What are we doing about Shatov?"

"We're working on it."

"Is that it?"

"That is it. I'll see you when you return."

So, we left thinking that we were letting Shatov and the other generals off the hook. Little did we know that this was only just the beginning. There would be more bloodshed and death before we finally came out the other end.

"I think we might call it a day there, gentlemen," Charles German said to us as he checked his watch.

I checked my own watch and saw we'd been at it for ten hours. Beside me, Knocker let out a long breath. I'd never seen him this patient before, and that included some of his outbursts.

Christine Ryan said, "I still have questions."

"They will have to wait until tomorrow when we reconvene." German looked at his folder, lifting papers and shuffling some others around. "I believe we will begin with the operation in the Congo."

"What time?" I asked.

"Eight?"

"I have a meeting in the morning," Holland said. "Can we make it nine?"

German ran his gaze over everyone in the room. "Any objections?"

None came.

"Then that will do it. You may go."

Knocker and I got up off our seats and stretched out the kinks. I suddenly felt exhausted. The days had been draining physically and mentally. We walked outside and Knocker said, "Fuck, Reaper, I'm glad that's over."

"Me, too," I agreed. "You feel like a beer?"

"Or six," he replied.

I slapped him on the shoulder. "Good. You buy."

"Bollocks."

A LOOK AT BOOK TWO:
CONGO ICE

The Democratic Republic of the Congo was in the middle of an uprising, and the Gods of War were behind it...

Kane and Jensen were determined to get to the bottom of whatever the generals were doing in the DRC but what started as a straightforward mission turned into something else entirely. Kinshasa was a warzone in which death was counted by the bodies in the streets. Outside the city was just as bad. The driving force was the Gods of War who needed all the diamonds the country had to offer.

Barely escaping with their lives, Kane and Jensen, along with Holly, head to Antwerp to spoil their plans. Instead, the streets ran red with blood as Antwerp became a new killing ground.

AVAILABLE JULY 2024

ABOUT THE AUTHOR

A relative newcomer to the world of writing, Brent Towns self-published his first book in 2015. Last Stand in Sanctuary took him two years to write. His first hardcover book, a Black Horse Western, was published the following year.

Since then, he has written twenty-six western stories, including some in collaboration with British western author, Ben Bridges; several action adventure novels, such as his bestselling Team Reaper series; the novelization to the 2019 movie, Bill Tilghman and the Outlaws; as well as scripted a handful of Commando Comics. Not bad for an Australian author, he thinks.

Often up until the small hours of the night, bashing away at his tortured keyboard in Queensland, Australia, Brent loves to lose himself in the world of fiction. If you're interested in sharing your thoughts in more detail, scan the QR code below! Your feedback is invaluable to him—and often helps shape his future writing endeavors.

www.ingramcontent.com/pod-product-compliance
Lightning Source LLC
La Vergne TN
LVHW030919080826
845145LV00013B/2973

* 9 7 8 1 6 8 5 4 9 3 5 7 8 *